D010082B

FAITH FOR THE FUTURE

When her teaching career in Paris comes to an unexpected end, Rosalind Mansell returns to the family farm in Shropshire. Faced with a number of family problems that greet her on arrival, the last thing on her mind is the possibility of a fresh relationship — especially when one of the new faces in the village belongs to the young vicar. After all, only elderly spinsters imagine themselves to be in love with the vicar . . . don't they?

KAREN ABBOTT

◆

FAITH FOR THE FUTURE

Complete and Unabridged

LINFORD
Leicester

First published in Great Britain in 2006

First Linford Edition
published 2007

British Library CIP Data

Abbott, Karen
    Faith for the future.—Large print ed.—
Linford romance library
    1. Love stories
    2. Large type books
    I. Title
    823.9'14 [F]

    ISBN 978–1–84617–679–1

Published by
F. A. Thorpe (Publishing)
Anstey, Leicestershire
Set by Words & Graphics Ltd.
Anstey, Leicestershire
Printed and bound in Great Britain by
T. J. International Ltd., Padstow, Cornwall

This book is printed on acid-free paper

1

Rosalind Mansell loved Paris . . . she had done so since her incredible luck in being granted a year's contract at an English-speaking school in the position of assistant teacher of geography. She had been here for almost nine months . . . and she didn't want to leave.

She leaned her arms on the top of the parapet that lined the banks of the River Seine at that point, drinking in the scene around her. The sun was shining; the flowers in the public parks were waving gently in the slight breeze; and carefree people were strolling along the river banks . . . couples arm-in-arm, lovers hand in hand, children skipping and others in solitary contemplation . . . all revelling in the warmth and the atmospheric ambience that could only be Paris.

Even in her troubled state of mind,

Ros wasn't oblivious to it. She lifted her face towards the sun and breathed in the heady perfume that floated on the breeze. She sighed with a mixture of longing and regret.

She had her own small apartment on the top floor of a tall, narrow town house that overlooked a small tree-lined square. On Saturdays and Sundays, she had breakfast in the pavement café across the street. Just a freshly-baked roll or a croissant and a cafetiere of coffee while she decided what to do that day.

She had made quite a few friends . . . but no-one special. Not unless she counted Jerome Brest. He had invited her out to dinner a few times and they had wandered around some art galleries together and poked among the second-hand shops looking for bargains.

At the thought of his name, her heart plummeted and the unbidden memory of a turbulent river flashed across her inner sight, replacing the tranquil Seine. She fought against the surging panic that threatened to overwhelm her; the memories of the shouts of alarm, the screams and the fruitless search. She felt again the despair and, this very afternoon, the voice of the college principal informing her that she was to be suspended until her future was decided by the official enquiry.

'What about monsieur Brest?' her faltering voice had asked. She had tried to get in touch with him, but her phone calls went unanswered and the concierge of his apartment block had repeatedly denied her access to the building.

The principal had frowned at her question. 'Monsieur Brest is under the same suspension order as yourself, but I firmly advise you not to make contact with him. It could jeopardise your case.'

He leaned forward, his expression softening slightly. 'Since the enquiry cannot take place until all the relevant information has been gathered, I have managed to persuade the judicial authorities to release your passport so that you may return to England for the time being, but you must return to Paris when you are summoned. Do you understand?'

Ros swallowed and nodded. 'Yes,' she had whispered.

'Good! Now, if you have no other questions, I must bid you au revoir.'

Ros stared at the river. What did the future hold for her? What if she could never teach again? Could she face it?

She thought of their mother, Eileen, coping almost single-handed with their family farm in Shropshire since Ted Mansell had walked out on his wife and three children five years ago.

He left a note to say he needed to get away; he needed a holiday. All they had had from him since were three post-cards; each one letting them know that he was all right and that they had no need to worry about him.

Huh! What about him worrying about them? How did he think their mum was managing without him? She got in extra help at busy times, such as lambing and harvest time ... when they could afford it ... but for the rest of the year, she managed, rarely letting slip her cheerful mask of, 'I'm coping fine.' ... and, thanks to the local church and community, they had.

With a surge of spirit, she straightened her shoulders and held high her head, as she turned her steps towards her apartment. She would not let this defeat her! She tucked a strand of her long blonde hair behind her left ear and smiled for the first time in days.

It was early evening when the telephone shrilled insistently into the subdued atmosphere of Ros's apartment, bringing a pause in the unwelcome task of sorting through her possessions. Her heart skipped a beat. What did they want now? She'd accepted their decision and agreed to leave quietly. Had they had second thoughts and now believed her version of events? Or maybe Jerome had changed his story? Was she to be reinstated?

Or . . . her heart began to beat erratically . . . was the caller Jerome? Was he about to break his self-imposed exile from her?

She snatched up the phone. 'Rosalind Mansell speaking.'

'Hi, Ros! It's me, Debbie!'

'Oh.' Ros's heart plummeted again as she recognised her sister's voice, but did her best to respond brightly. 'Hi, Debs! How are you?'

'Er . . . I'm fine,' her sister said in hesitant accents that at once alerted Ros that this was more than a casual phone call.

'What's wrong?'

'It's Mum, I'm afraid.'

Debbie's voice was shaky and Ros's heart began to pound.

'What's the matter?' she asked, her fear of bad news making her voice sharper than she intended.

'It's not as bad as we feared at first,' Debbie said quickly. 'She's had a heart attack and she's in hospital.'

'Oh, Debs! When did it happen?'

Ros's voice rose in her anxiety. She couldn't bear to think of their mum wired up to a spaghetti-junction of tubes. She was an outdoor woman. Hale and hearty, a hard-working farmer in her own right, who'd never had a day's illness in her life.

'It was first thing this morning. I've only just got back home. Andrew closed the restaurant and saw to the farm. He said he'll do the same tomorrow, but I can't let him keep doing that. I'll have to get something organised. I just wondered . . . I know you've just had your Whitsun holiday . . . but . . . ' Debbie's voice petered out.

Ros knew at once what she had to say. The pub would soon lose its customers if they kept closing the place. People expected them to be open at all hours! And they had two young children to take into consideration.

'Don't worry! I'll come home straight away,' she said quickly.

'Are you sure? Oh, that is a relief! Of course, Nick volunteered to stay off school. He would! Even though he says he doesn't like farming, I think he likes school even less!'

Ros's brain whirled round in double-quick time. She would have to arrange to leave Paris sooner than she had anticipated, but maybe that was just as well, under the present circumstances. It would only be a temporary measure, of course, until they knew more about how their mum would be . . . but it was an answer to her own dilemma as well.

'It's all right! I'll get things sorted out here as quickly as I can and, hopefully, I'll be with you in a couple of days. Is that all right?'

'As long as you're sure?' Debbie's voice portrayed both her relief and her doubt. 'I don't want you to risk losing your job, love. You know Mum wouldn't want that!'

'It's all right, Debs. Don't worry! Give Mum my love when you see her again and tell her I'll be at Rainbow's End as soon as I can.'

It was three days later when Ros

arrived at Manchester Airport and took the shuttle bus into the city centre. There, she booked a single rail ticket to Shrewsbury.

Thankfully, Debbie had reported that their mother was making satisfactory progress, but Ros knew it would be a long haul until she was fit enough to manage the farm on her own again. However much Ros was glad to be able to come home at this moment of need, she knew that farming wasn't, and never would be, the love of her life. They would need to have a family meeting to discuss what was to be done long-term.

A couple of line repairs and missed connections made the journey seem interminable and the dark clouds that had been building up through the afternoon decided to let down their contents with a vengeance just as the train pulled into Shrewsbury station.

Ros wished she had phoned ahead to ask Debbie if she could arrange for someone to come to collect her, but she hadn't wanted to add any pressure to her sister's already busy schedule . . . and there was the last taxi just pulling out of the rank.

Oh, no! It would take forever on the bus! Hang on a bit! Wasn't that Martin Felton over there? She hadn't known him very well . . . only briefly at village shows and such like, but his family home, Melford Manor, was barely a mile out of Melford Green, the village where she lived. In fact, the manor and the farm had adjoining land.

Martin was striding purposefully towards the other entrance, looking for all the world as if he were expecting to meet someone. Maybe Debbie had fixed her a lift after all?

Her face lighting up, she stepped forward, calling, 'Martin!'

The screech of brakes just behind her, made her leap round in alarm and she found herself almost leaning over the bonnet of a car. The handle of her smaller suitcase had been pulled out of her hand and the case was now pressed between the car's bumper and her left leg. Thoroughly shaken, she stared aghast at the ashen face of the driver through the windscreen. He was young, late-twenties to early-thirties, she guessed and he looked more shaken than angry.

He leaped out of the car and hastened towards her.

'Are you all right?' he asked sharply, seeming to tower over her. His hair was very dark and, with the rain now plastering it to his skull, it seemed like a shiny black cap.

He reached out his hand but Ros grabbed at the handle of her suitcase and took a step backwards, only prevented from going farther by the fact that her suitcase seemed to be wedged under the number plate.

'No thanks to you!' she shot back at him, feeling alarmed by his gesture towards her. Her agitation made her respond in attack. 'Do you always drive like a maniac?' she snapped.

'You did unexpectedly step in front of me,' the man mildly pointed out, his composure softening as he realised that she was unhurt, but badly shaken.

'Nonsense! I . . . '

Ros stopped, suddenly aware that she was standing at least a stride away from the edge of the pavement. Oh, dear!

Her shoulders sagged. 'I'm sorry,' she said apologetically. 'I saw someone I know. I thought he might . . . ' She looked around as she spoke, hoping that Martin was coming to her aid, but there was no sign of him. 'Oh, he's gone.'

She bit her lower lip, suddenly feeling very foolish and at a distinct disadvantage. The rain was pouring down on them both. She was wet, cold and tired and she had almost caused a serious accident. The thought of that thoroughly threw her. Causing accidents seemed to be the only thing she was particularly good at, at the moment!

An impatient car driver tooted his horn and Ros hastily looked around, realising that they were blocking the turning-round space. 'I'm sorry!' she repeated, trying to tug her suitcase free of the car bumper and number plate. 'I'll get out of your way.'

'Look, can I be of any help?' the man offered. 'I've just dropped off a passenger for the train.' He spread his hands expansively, vaguely indicating towards his car, a rather battered black Honda. 'Can I give you a lift somewhere?'

Still feeling as panic-stricken as a rabbit caught in the glare of a car's headlights at night, Ros was almost mesmerised by his twinkling eyes. They were the colour of rich treacle, she decided, the thought making her taste buds sense the smooth, mellow flavour of the treacle toffee her mother always made for bonfire night.

She swiftly regained control of her spiralling emotions. 'No! No! I wouldn't dream of it!' she stammered, backing away. Heavens! That was all she needed. With her present track record, she'd be getting into the car of the local Bluebeard! 'No! I don't know you! You could be anyone!'

The man grinned. 'I'm quite respect-able. In fact I'm . . . '

'I don't care who you are!'

All Ros wanted was to get as far away from him as possible and forget the whole embarrassment! To her relief, a taxi turned into the area and she immediately hailed it.

'I'll take the taxi,' she said in desperation, thankful that a final tug at her suitcase set it free, enabling her to turn away from the man and drag her two suitcases towards the stationary taxi. All she wanted to do was get away from here and go home!

The taxi driver swiftly took her suitcases and put them inside the boot and Ros got into the back seat. She leaned her head back against the headrest and closed her eyes.

'I think the young man you were with wants you,' the taxi driver mentioned as he slid into his seat.

'Pardon?'

Ros stared through the window. Sure

enough, the man as striding towards the taxi, his hand raised.

'Drive on!' she commanded curtly, adding by way of explanation, 'I'm afraid he was pestering me.' Her cheeks flamed as she spoke the words, knowing them to be untrue, but she felt unable to face any more confrontation with the man.

She gave the driver her destination and leaned back once more, thankful to be able to leave the remainder of her journey in other hands. It had seemed a long day. Her mind drifted and she was unaware of how much time had passed when the driver spoke again, meeting her eyes in the reflection of his driving mirror.

'He's following us, that fellow is, Miss. What d'you want me to do? He's flashing his lights at us.'

Wearily, Ros looked over her shoulder through the rear window. The sight of the black Honda with its headlights flashing aroused an unreasonable anger within her. Had the man nothing better to do than to persecute her? Sure, she had nearly flung herself under his car . . . but surely he realised that it was merely an unfortunate slip of attention on her part!

'Stop the car!' she snapped. 'What he needs is a good piece of my mind!'

Regardless of the still-pouring rain, she angrily wrenched the door open and leaped out, not even giving thought to what she was going to say. She marched up to the Honda and stood by the driver's door, her hands on her hips, deliberately not giving him enough space to open his door and get out. Let him feel the discomfort of someone towering over him for a change!

He wound down his window and gave a smile of greeting . . . which only served to increase her fury.

'How dare you follow me like this? Are you some kind of nutcase or something? Well, let me tell you that I've taken note of your number plate and if I catch sight of you anywhere within twenty metres of me again I won't hesitate to report you to the police! Is that clear?'

The young man listened silently, making no effort to defend himself. His quiet demeanour slowly took the heat out of Ros's anger and left her hovering uncertainly.

'Right!' she added, now unsure what to say next. 'As long as you've got that clear, maybe you'll back off? OK?'

Her eyes were drawn to his slightly twisted humorous smile and she felt her insides quiver as his lips parted to show his even white teeth, reminding her of how attractive he was. Even so, a warm flush began to cover her cheeks and she raised her eyes to meet his, but immediately wished that she hadn't. The pleasant twinkle that had been there now seemed to have been replaced by a hint of mockery.

'As you wish, Miss . . . er . . . '

'Oh, no. You don't get my name that easily. I'm not that stupid!'

The man's eyebrows twitched, as if

questioning that assertion. Without speaking a word, he reached over to his passenger seat and picked something up, turning back towards Ros.

A fleeting moment of alarm as she wondered if he were about to produce a gun and attempt to kidnap her or something equally preposterous, was swiftly replaced by acute embarrassment. Dangling from the man's hand was her shoulder bag . . . an item that she didn't even know she had lost! Her money was in it and her passport.

'Oh!'

His eyebrows twitched again. 'Precisely.'

Her face flamed. This was going from bad to worse. She swallowed hard and reached out her hand.

'Thank you,' she said stiffly. 'I seem to have misjudged your actions.'

The man smiled, a little tightly, it now seemed, but she could hardly blame him, could she?

'Your apology is accepted,' he said quietly.

He raised his hand in salute, wound up his window and indicated that he was going to overtake the taxi. Ros hastily stepped aside and watched as he drove off down the road without a backward glance.

'Hateful man!' she snapped irrationally and stormed back to her taxi. How totally humiliated he had made her feel! She sincerely hoped that she would never set eyes on him again!

2

It was a relief to finally arrive at the farm. The rain had stopped and she paid the taxi off at the main gate, where she was noisily welcomed by their two dogs, Tiger and Ben. She fondled their ears and then laughingly pushing the dogs down. Debbie came out to see what the rumpus was about and the two sisters had an emotional reunion.

'It's so good to have you home!' Debbie assured her, holding her at arms' length to appraise her. 'Now, come on inside. Tea's nearly ready.'

Ros glanced around, looking for their fifteen-year-old brother. 'Is Nick home? maybe he could help me with some of my bags? Or is he helping Andrew with the milking?'

'No, he isn't here, neither of them are. Nick said he was meeting some friends in town after school and Andrew had some business to attend to. Hugh Tipton's doing the milking.'

Ros couldn't help expressing surprise. 'Hugh Tipton? Is that a good idea? You know Mum doesn't like him very much.'

Debbie flushed at the implied criticism. 'Maybe she doesn't, but she had to ask someone to help her! He's been helping her off and on for quite a while now. I couldn't do more than I have been doing. It's bad enough having the pub to run and Natasha and Amy to look after.'

Ros was taken aback by Debbie's tone. 'I'm sorry. I didn't mean to criticise. It's just, well, Hugh never does anything for nothing, does he? What's he after?'

Debbie shrugged. 'I don't know, maybe he's just being a good neighbour at last. He seemed pretty keen to help when Mum first asked him and it just seemed to be the best thing to do to ask him to be in charge when Mum was rushed into hospital.'

Ros linked her hand through Debbie's arm. 'Well, I'm glad I'm here to help now. Is Hugh managing on his own, then?'

'I've been doing a bit, but he said to leave it to him today to give you a chance to settle in and so that you can go and see Mum tonight.'

The kitchen was a large, homely room. A huge Aga dominated one wall and on the adjacent wall was a chest of drawers laden with various farming catalogues, magazines and other paperwork and a large dresser that held a rich array of blue and white crockery.

Two cats, Ginger and Pickle, were curled up on the windowsill, basking in the sunshine.

Ros sniffed the air appreciatively. 'It smells good! I didn't realise how hungry I am!'

Debbie's cheeks coloured at the praise. 'You can eat it now, if you like. If Nick's not home soon he'll have to make do with his meal kept warm. I've made a steak and kidney pie. I hope that's all right for you.'

'It sounds fine! Just what I need. Don't worry about Nick. I don't suppose it'll be the first time he's been late for a meal! Is he still giving Mum a bit of grief?'

Debbie pulled a face. 'And some! Mum says he's got in with the wrong crowd at school. I'll skin him alive if he gets into more trouble while Mum's in hospital. Honestly, he's got no consideration!'

Ros shrugged. 'He's a lad!' she said lightly, not wanting to be drawn into an argument about their brother so soon after arriving home. 'What time's visiting?'

'Half-past seven. You'll be able to manage the Land Rover, won't you?'

'I expect so. It's like a bit like riding a bike, isn't it?'

Debbie suddenly turned to Ros and impulsively hugged her again. 'I'm sorry if I sounded a bit grumpy, Ros. I didn't mean to be. It's just that it's been like running two businesses

. . . but, now you're back with us, everything will be all right again.'

★ ★ ★

In the nearby town, Nick Mansell squirmed uncomfortably under Gary Welling's scornful gaze.

Ryan Thomas, the other of his two main associates at school, in spite of an inane grin, was looking uneasily from one to the other, obviously wondering which side to take.

'It'll be easy!' Gary boasted. 'All you have to do is wait until I've distracted the old geezer and then grab a handful of CDs and run! You've done it in the newsagent's! So, what's the problem?'

'It was only a Mars Bar from Bridgman's. CDs are worth more!' Nick protested. He didn't want to lose face, but he hadn't expected it to get this far. He had fearfully spent all week expecting that dreaded knock at the door and had flinched every time the phone rang.

'That's the whole point, stupid!' Gary scoffed. 'Right, Ryan, you'd better do it first! Show this softie how it's done!'

'What?' Ryan looked uncertain now the spotlight was on him. 'Yeh, OK, then! But you'd best keep the bloke busy! My dad'll wallop me if I'm caught!'

Gary raised his eyes skyward. 'Are you doing it or not?'

'Yeh, OK,' Ryan agreed. He turned to Nick. 'Watch this!'

The two boys sauntered into the shop. Ryan halted by the CD stand and Gary went over to the pay desk and engaged the shopkeeper in some sort of conversation.

Nick watched anxiously. He ought to have been home ages ago. Thank goodness it was Debbie making his tea. Mum would have known immediately that he'd been up to no good. A surge of adrenalin flowed as he saw Ryan grab a handful of CDs and leg it out of the shop towards him.

'Run!' Ryan shouted.

Nick froze momentarily . . . until Ryan thrust the CDs at him and pushed him into action. With no more ado, Nick swung about and charged after Ryan, only realising he was holding the CDs when they had rounded a corner and sagged against the wall to get their breath back.

'Is anyone following us?' Ryan asked.

Nick poked his head gingerly around the corner. 'I don't think so.'

'Good!' He grabbed back the CDs. 'I'll have these back now. you can get some of your own tomorrow afternoon.'

Nick's heart was beating fast. 'I'm not . . . '

'Not what?' Gary's voice demanded behind him, his face thrust terrifyingly near to his. 'Not still chicken, are you?'

'N . . . no!'

'Well, d'you want to be in our gang or not? You may as well say now because there's loads of others lined up waiting to join!'

'Yeh, 'course I do! I've said so, haven't I?'

'Right! Half past three tomorrow afternoon . . . here! And don't be late! Come on, Ryan. Let's go and listen to them,' nodding towards the CDs. 'See you tomorrow, Nick!'

'Yeh, right!'

With false bravado, Nick turned and left them and, unconsciously imitating Gary's swagger, set off towards the bus station. He hadn't gone far when a car drew up at the side of him and the driver leaned over and wound down the window.

'Hello, Nick! I thought it was you! Want a lift home?'

Nick started guiltily and felt his face blush hotly as he recognised the new vicar who had recently moved into Melford Green.

'Oh, hello. I'm sorry. I didn't see you,' he mumbled. Had he seen what they'd been doing? Did vicars have a hotline to God? He hoped not!

Paul Ashley merely smiled. 'Hop in,

27

then,' he invited, opening the passenger door.

Nick glanced down the street, but couldn't think of a way to refuse a lift without raising Paul's suspicions, so he sat in the passenger seat and busied himself fastening the seat belt.

'How are you managing at the farm?' Paul asked as he slid into first gear. 'If there's anything I can do . . . ' He left the sentence unfinished, concentrating on his driving.

'That's all right. My other sister, Ros, is due home today,' Nick was glad to inform him, not wanting the vicar to have too much free access to his home. He didn't fancy being the object of anyone's social conscience, though he conceded that, as far as vicars went, Paul wasn't too bad.

'Ah, yes! Your mother had mentioned it the other day. I'd forgotten,' Paul replied. 'Coming home today, you say? Er . . . what does she look like?'

Nick shrugged. 'She's fairly tall with

long blonde hair. I s'pose she's pretty . . . sort of.'

Nick glanced sideways and was surprised to see that the young vicar had lost some of his composure. There was even the hint of a rise in colour on his cheekbones. Don't say he was girl-shy! What a laugh!

Lost in his morose thoughts, Nick made a poor travelling companion and he was glad when the car pulled up by the main gate of Rainbow's End Farm. He scrambled out of the car with mumbled thanks and climbed over the gate, barely noticing the rapturous welcome the dogs gave him.

Paul wound down the window and watched the lad as he slouched through the farmyard. 'Tell your sister I'll look forward to seeing her in church on Sunday!' he called after him. 'And you, of course, as well!'

Nick barely acknowledged his call and Paul wound up the window and slipped into first gear. He frowned slightly, more than a little perturbed by the lad's sullen attitude. What had Nick and his friends been up to? He had looked a little furtive when he offered him a lift.

Then he laughed. All fifteen-year-old boys look furtive when spotted by the vicar! He thought again about what Nick had said about his sister. Ros, eh? He grinned to himself. Now, that should be an interesting meeting!

Saturday dawned bright and sunny and Ros swiftly washed and then dressed in a pair of old jeans and T-shirt eager to make a start. She wondered whether or not to go and awaken Nick and insist that he join her, but didn't want to come down too heavily on him. She'd make sure he was ready to help on Sunday, though, so that she could go to church afterwards, keen to re-establish the familiar pattern of life in the village whilst she was here.

The cats twined themselves around her legs and followed her outside. Tiger came along too and she let Ben out of his kennel. He leapt around like the frisky two-year-old that he was.

'Get down, you daft dog!' Ros protested, laughing at his antics. His ears cocked over and met in the middle but he had a bright intelligent face. He'd be a good worker once he was fully trained.

Hugh had let out the hens and ducks from their overnight bondage, she noticed, and he had already started the milking when she reached the milking parlour. He looked up at her without a smile.

'You're late! Yer mam allus fetches the cows in fer me to milk 'em!' he said sourly. 'Mind you, 'er oughtn't be having to do all this, your mam oughtn't! it be too much for her — kill her in the end, it will, you mark my words! Too much for a maid like you, as well!'

'I'm sure you mean well, Mr Tipton, but such talk would only upset my mother,' Ros said as lightly as she could, not wanting to upset him unnecessarily.

'Well, 'er needs to think about it!' Hugh muttered, as if to himself as he jotted down the yield and moved the milking tackle along to the next position. 'Someone needs to think about it before the farm ends in wrack and ruin!'

'I'm sure we'll manage,' Ros said brightly, 'It's been good of you to step in like this and Mum said how grateful she is, when I saw her last night.'

'Just being neighbourly,' Hugh returned, 'and the money comes in handy,' he added, as if he feared Ros might think his neighbourliness went as far as working without payment.

Ros went down to the other end of the parlour and, after checking the cow's identity tag and consulting the list on the wall, she began with the second set of milking machinery.

She mulled Hugh's words over as she worked her way down the row of cows. Would her mum consider easing up? Selling the herd, maybe?

Ros knew that a few decisions would

have to be made soon, but, at least her own problems could be left on a back-burner for a while, she reflected wryly.

Back at the farm, she eased off her wellies outside the outer kitchen door and stepped over Tiger, who was now sprawled across the middle of the porch, his tail thumping the ground at her approach.

It wasn't long before the smell of bacon cooking drifted upstairs and roused Nick. He was dressed in his working clothes, she noted with relief, and, over breakfast, she detailed some of the jobs to be done that day.

'Have the hen and duck cabins been cleaned since Mum went into hospital?'

'I haven't had time,' he began defensively.

'I'm not saying you should have had time. I'm just asking. Have they been done?'

Nick scowled at her.

'Not as far as I know!'

'Right, they need doing today.'

'I've arranged to meet Ryan and Gary in town this afternoon.'

'That's OK. We should have finished by then.' She played with her pen before looking up and fixing her eyes on Nick. 'I need you to pull your weight, you know, Nick. I've been away for so long. I need you to tell me what needs doing. I don't want to be asking Mum all the time, she needs a thorough rest.'

'She will get better, won't she?'

Ros saw the pain of anxiety in his eyes and her heart softened. 'Yes, of course she will. But she can't go straight back into doing all the heavy work, if ever. Things will have to change a bit. We'll all have to do a bit more until we get things sorted.'

She was relieved when Nick got up from the table with no further demur and set off to do the jobs she'd delegated. He even whistled the dogs to go with him.

It wasn't long before she was following after him. The path from the house to the hen cabins went alongside a babbling stream that gurgled its way along this, the outer border of their land at this point. Somehow, its repetitive, eternal sound was soothing.

'Come on! Come on!' she called encouragingly to the scattered hens as she walked down the path, unconsciously echoing her mother's tones that she had grown up hearing. Hens appeared from everywhere, leaving their more laborious pecking and scratching the ground for this, their daily treat.

Nick had already cast around an assortment of plastic lids from a variety of large food containers and on to these she dropped a handful of mash, laughing as the hens eagerly scrambled for prime pecking space.

Nick was busy cleaning out the triangular-prism-shaped duck houses, so Ros made her way to the hen cabins, armed with a pitchfork to drag out the old straw and a bucket of water and scrubbing brush to clean the perches.

It must have been about half-an-hour later when the sound of the dogs barking drew her out of a hen cabin. She strolled to where she could see up the farmyard to the gate. A visitor had arrived. As she watched, he sprang out of the car and went to shut the gate securely.

Ros called out, 'Hello! We're down here!'

The man hesitated and then swung towards her. As he drew nearer, Ros could see it was Martin Felton, casually dressed in jeans, light sweater and open fleece jacket.

Glancing down at her soiled working clothes, Ros felt at a distinct disadvantage.

'Ros! Great to see you again!' Martin greeted her, advancing with his hand outstretched. His face, whilst not of classic handsomeness, was pleasantly good-looking and he wore his light brown hair at a short length.

Ros wiped her hand on the seat of her jeans and allowed him to grasp hold of it. 'Hello, Martin!' she answered, unable to keep a note of surprise out of her voice. 'Is this a social visit . . . or business?'

'Social, of course!' he smiled down at her.

'How did you know I was home?' Ros queried. 'Did you see me at the station yesterday? I was at the taxi rank, but none were available.'

For a fleeting second, Martin looked disconcerted but he swiftly rallied. 'Sorry! You have me there! I was . . . making a timetable enquiry. You should have called me. Did you get a taxi?'

'Eventually, yes. But, if you didn't see me at the station, how did you know I was home? And why . . . ?'

'Why have I hot-footed it to your door to make you welcome?' Martin looked slightly embarrassed but grinned disarmingly. 'Well, if I'm to be truly honest, I'm here at the bequest of my father.'

'Geoffrey? Why?'

'He's in his 'squire of the village' mode, I'm afraid. Got to encourage solidarity of the community, etc.'

Ros eyed him suspiciously. 'Why? Are local elections due?'

Martin laughed. 'I don't think so, but I wouldn't put it past the old codger to be looking to the future! But, no, he just pressed me into service to welcome you home and pass on the family's regards to you all concerning your mother's illness.'

'Thank you. That was kind of him. Now, I don't want to be un-neighbourly, but I've got tons to do.'

He laughed self-consciously and then his expression sobered and he reached out and plucked a length of straw out of Ros's hair. 'But, on my own behalf, Ros, I'd like to take you out for a drink one night . . . if that's all right with you.'

Ros hesitated. She wasn't sure she wanted male company just now. Jerome's defection hadn't left her unscathed. Her intention to refuse must have shown on her face because Martin quickly said, 'It would be of great service to me.

Father wants me to take more part in community affairs.'

He looked so earnest about it that Ros hadn't the heart to turn him down. 'Yes. That would be nice,' she agreed. 'Only not tonight! I'm just home and I need to get myself sorted.'

She fancied she saw a fleeting flicker of relief flash across Martin's face and she wondered why he had issued the invitation, but then he grinned disarmingly.

'Right! We'll put it on hold for a day or so, but don't think you can wriggle out of it now you've agreed!'

Ros watched him depart . . . then her thoughts returned to the work in hand. There was a lot to do and, when she finally lay in her bed that night, she realised that she hadn't given Jerome Brest a single thought that day and her turmoil over the possible outcome of the distant enquiry had eased a great deal.

The Sunday morning milking followed the pattern of Saturday. Nick, having declined to go to church, had agreed to collect the eggs when he got himself out of bed and Ros happily got changed, looking forward to meeting other villagers.

Her progress into church was slow and it was only the appearance of the church warden with his staff that urged her to hurry into a pew before the choir and vicar began their procession down the aisle. Busily finding her place in the service book, she only looked up when the voice of the vicar announced the first hymn.

No! It couldn't be!

She closed her eyes, hoping the image would be different when she looked again, but it wasn't! The man in clerical grab was none other than the man who had offered her a lift on Friday! The man she had more or less accused of following her with suspicious intent!

3

Ros knew her face had flamed crimson and took comfort in the fact that she was seated well back from the pulpit. In fact, if she moved a foot to her right when she stood up to sing, she would be partly concealed behind a stone pillar.

What was he doing here? Where was Reverend Walsh and his family? Instead of singing a hymn, she wracked her brains and unearthed vague memories of her mother writing to tell her of an exchange that had been made because of some specialist medical treatment Reverend Walsh's younger son needed. Well, how was she to have remembered?

For what she took in of the service, she may as well have stayed at home. She sighed with resignation as the service drew to its close. Best get it over with. Even so, when the choir processed down the aisle with the vicar in their wake, Ros busied herself by delving into her shoulder bag, hoping to avoid recognition.

Trying to merge with other members of the congregation as the line slowly approached the figure in the doorway of the main porch, Ros squared her shoulders, took a deep breath, assuming a carefree expression on her face. She held out her hand when it was her turn to be greeted.

'Good morning, er . . . Ah!'

The broad smile that lit his face on seeing her would melt the coldest of hearts. His dark eyes seemed to be filled with laughter.

Ros forced herself not to respond too readily. Still smarting from their meeting on Friday, she was in no mood to be captivated by a show of friendliness. The warmth in his dark brown eyes almost persuaded her otherwise.

They gave the instant impression of trustworthiness and caused a tiny spiral of anticipation of pleasure to flare into life deep within her.

Time seemed to stand still and Ros was brought back to reality when Miss Pepper, the postmistress, spoke at her side. 'Oh, you won't know Ros, will you Paul? She's Eileen Mansell's daughter, heroically come home especially to look after her mother and help her run the family farm. Haven't you, dear?'

Ros smiled weakly, inwardly shrinking from the word, *heroically*. She wondered if the deception she was allowing by her tacit agreement of Miss Pepper's assessment of her homecoming . . . for how could she correct it in so public a place? . . . would show on her face.

'I'm delighted to make your acquaintance, Ros,' he said easily, his eyes still dancing. 'Your mother mentioned your imminent arrival on my latest visit to see her. I'm so glad you could get leave of absence from your teaching post. I know it means a lot to Eileen.'

He was still holding her hand and Ros somehow didn't want him to let go.

However, she was determined to remain cool, even though her senses felt as if she were suffering from a mild form of intoxication. She mentally shook herself and forced herself to speak.

'Thank you, Reverend . . . '

'Ashley,' he supplied, adding, 'but call me Paul. I don't stand on too formal a footing with my parishioners. After all, we're part of one large family, aren't we?' His eyes took on a more serious hue as he added, 'Here to stand by each other and help wherever there is a need.'

Her heart thumped alarmingly. Did his words have a hidden meaning? Ros wondered if he could somehow read into her soul . . . as if he knew that something were amiss. But, no, that was impossible.

'Maybe I'll see you again at tonight's service? I'm hoping to offer a more informal type of evening worship once or twice a month. Maybe you could come along and give me your opinion of it?'

'Oh, I . . . '

'Sorry, Paul. Ros is already claimed for this evening,' a male voice spoke by her right ear and a hand was laid on her arm, drawing her hand at last out of Paul's grasp.

Feeling cut adrift, Ros turned to see who it was and saw Martin Felton at her side, smiling down with a proprietary air. 'Isn't that right, Ros? I've booked a table at the Four Crosses for half-past eight. 'Bye, Paul.'

Martin was steering her outside as he spoke and, short of causing a fuss, Ros felt compelled to go with him, with only time to fling an apologetic glance over her shoulder towards the new vicar as she went, hoping he didn't think her abysmally ill-mannered.

'I didn't agree to come out with you!' she hissed at Martin as soon as they were out of earshot. 'Anyway, there's all the farm work to do!'

'I'm sure you did!' Martin smiled. 'And, anyway, I had to rescue you from our eager new vicar, didn't I? And you'll be glad of a chance to relax. You'll have finished milking by half-past seven and I'm sure Hugh will clean up for you.'

Ros pulled away from him, not sure she wanted to be organised like this. 'You seem to know all about us.'

Martin smiled and shrugged. 'It's a village. Everyone knows what everyone else is doing.' He squeezed her arm. 'I'll pick you up at eight, then.'

'All right,' she agreed. Then, ashamed of her lack of enthusiasm, she flashed him a bright smile. 'Thanks, Martin. I'll look forward to it.'

Martin strode down the path with a casual back-wave of his hand and Ros saw him acknowledge various greetings from different villagers as he made for his car — a flamboyant red open sports car.

Hearing a call of, 'Hello, there!' Ros looked around and saw Joanna Stansbury, the owner of the local riding school who rented some land from Rainbow's End, waving her arm. She returned the wave and took a step towards her, ready to exchange some chat, but when she realised that Joanna had been calling to Martin, not her, she turned away and was soon caught up in giving the latest report on her mother's progress to other villagers.

It was a close-knit community and Ros received many more goodwill messages to pass on to Eileen. When she glanced back at the church porch, Paul Ashley had gone and Ros escaped homeward as soon as she was able.

The Four Crosses was further afield than most Melford Green villagers went for a casual evening out and so they saw no-one Ros knew. She wasn't too surprised. She had been out of local circulation for over four years and had no idea where any of her contemporaries would have chosen to go.

It was a pleasant evening and although Martin was openly flirting with her, he didn't seem too put out when she nimbly evaded his attempt to draw her into his arms when he pulled up once more outside the farm gate.

'Thanks! It's been a great evening!' she said lightly as she opened the car door and slipped out before he could stop her.

Martin laughed ruefully. 'My pleasure,' he said gallantly. 'We must do it again . . . soon. I'll call you.'

Nick surprised her by being home before her and she was gratified by his offer to get up early and do some chores before setting off for school the following day.

'You can make me a plate of eggs and bacon instead,' he said, grinning at her comical expression of surprise, 'and some sandwiches for lunch. Agreed?'

'Agreed!' replied Ros, slapping his raised hand with her own. It seemed her little brother was taking some share of responsibility after all.

The following morning, the bacon was sizzling nicely and the eggs were in a saucer ready to slide into the frying pan when she was alerted to the fact that something was wrong by the sight of Nick running back up the farmyard, his face twisted by some heaving of emotion.

Ros hurried to the kitchen door, nearly falling over Tiger who was struggling to get to his feet, also aware of some crisis. 'Nick! What is it?'

'Oh, Ros! They're dead! All of them!'

'Who's dead?' Ros gasped, reaching out to enfold him in her arms. She couldn't remember when she had last seen Nick so upset — when their dad had left, she supposed.

'The ducks! All of them! Feathers everywhere! Oh, it's awful, Ros! The hut's like a slaughter house! Hugh says it's my fault. He said I mustn't have checked properly last night . . . or not shut the door properly. But I did, Ros! I did!'

'Of course you did!' She patted his head against her chest, as she would comfort a child, momentarily closing her eyes, imagining the scene. 'It will be a stoat that's done it. They don't need much of a gap to get in, you know that.'

Nick hiccupped against her and then drew away, wiping his face with the back of his hand. 'It's horrible! They must have been terrified out of their wits,' he burst out. 'I hate farming. I don't care what Mum says. I'm not doing it! I hate the killing!!'

The anguish in his voice tore at her heart. She wanted to draw him into her arms again, but could tell he didn't want that. Instead, she quickly made him a mug of tea, thankful that the kettle was always on the boil at this time of day, and made him sit down at the table.

'Drink that, Nick. Here, stir some sugar into it. You've had a nasty shock.'

'They'll have to be cleared away,' Nick said dully. He pushed the untouched mug of tea away from him and started to stand up, his face white.

Ros gently pushed him down again. 'I'll see to it. Drink your tea.'

It was a terrible sight. Utter carnage. Suddenly, she couldn't face it. She shut the door abruptly and leaned against it, her eyes closed as she tried to erase the image, until she became aware that someone was close by and opened her eyes to see Hugh Tipton peering at her, a leering sort of satisfaction in his expression.

'Yon lad's no farmer,' he said dourly, shaking his head. 'Turned green, he did! Got to expect things like this when you farm with animals, see. Like I said to your mam last week, it's time she gets out while she can, whilst the land's in good order. I wouldn't mind a couple of fields myself, if we can agree a good price, that is.'

'We have no intention of selling our land, Mr Tipton,' Ros said tightly. 'And I really think you ought to have more sensitivity than to be talking about it right now. Nick had a nasty shock.'

She ran back to the farmhouse. Nick wasn't in the kitchen. She ran upstairs and knocked gently on the door to his room. She heard a grunt of some sort and pushed open the door. Nick was sitting disconsolately on the end of his bed staring blankly through the window.

'I've missed the school bus to town,' he said flatly.

'I think you should still go, if you can face it. I tell you what, why don't you take the cows to river meadow and I'll finish making our breakfast. Then I'll run you to school in the Land Rover.'

That worked out quite well and it was still short of ten o'clock when Ros was once more driving into the village on her way home. As she approached the end of the vicarage drive, Paul Ashley appeared. He instantly recognised her vehicle and waved his hand, indicating to her to stop. She drew up and wound down her window.

Paul stepped round the vehicle. 'I'm sorry to hear of the mishap this morning.'

Ros couldn't help smiling, albeit a little grimly. 'I'd forgotten how fast the jungle telegraph works. Who told you?'

'I was in the village store when Hugh Tipton was telling Mrs Barclay. Is there anything I can do? It can't be pleasant, especially when you know the creatures involved.'

'I didn't know them well, but you're right, it's not pleasant. However, needs must.'

Paul's eyes were soft and warm as they searched her face, bringing her emotions perilously near the surface. Not wanting to break down in front of him, Ros turned away and slipped into first gear. Paul reached through the open window and touched her arm.

'Don't feel you have to face it yourself, Ros. You're a capable young woman, from what your mother says, but you can't carry the world on your shoulders. If you'll allow me to, I'll come with you and do what's neces-sary.'

It was on the tip of her tongue to refuse, but the compassion in his voice made her hesitate. She remembered her hasty refusal of his previous offer of help. Not wanting to dwell too much on that, she found herself saying, 'Will you? Are you sure? I would appreciate it.'

Thankfully, Paul didn't talk during the short journey and, once at the farm, Ros pointed him in the right direction. He swiftly summed up the situation, helped himself to a couple of sacks from the corner of the first barn and went to the silent, closed-up duck-house. Ros left him to it, preferring to busy herself in the kitchen, clearing away the breakfast dishes and checking that there was enough water in the kettle to make a hot drink.

By the time Paul came to the kitchen, she was buttering some pieces of toast. Her hand hovered over the kettle.

'Would you like a drink? Tea or coffee?'

'Coffee, please . . . and that toast smells good!'

'I've done some for you. Help yourself.'

She found Paul easy to talk to. He listened as well as talked and seemed to understand things that were unsaid.

Still, that was his job, she reflected, trying to distance herself from the warmth of his understanding.

'Mum will be upset,' she murmured inconsequently.

'Have you got any of their eggs?'

'I expect so . . . in fact, yes, I know we've got some in the fridge.'

'Could you incubate some?'

Ros stared blankly . . . then understanding dawned. 'Of course! Why didn't I think of that? Do you think there's a chance?'

'I don't see why not. You had some male ducks, didn't you? The eggs will be fertilised.'

'But they've been in the fridge for some days.'

'I've heard of it happening. Have you got an incubator?'

'No. I'll need to contact the Egg Marketing Board. We usually hire one from them.'

'You do that . . . and, if they have one, I'll pop over and collect it.'

'It's very kind of you.' Ros looked at

him almost shyly. 'Er, I'm . . . I'm sorry about the way I behaved on Friday. I was . . . '

' . . . at the end of a long tiring day and anxious about your mother.'

'Yes.'

'Think no more about it. I am used to seeing people who are suffering extremes of emotion. It goes with the job.'

Ros smiled at him gratefully, hastily revising her first impressions of him. 'You're a nice man.'

Later, Ros almost squirmed with embarrassment when she recalled what she had said to him. 'You're a nice man,' indeed! What must he think of her? Still, as a vicar, he was supposed to be nice, wasn't he?

The jungle drums must have carried on beating. A few farmers' wives telephoned and, just before lunch, Martin came. 'Just heard about your fiasco this morning. Anything I can do?'

'It's all been done . . . but thanks for offering. Paul came and cleared it all away for me. He's gone to pick up an incubator from Shrewsbury.'

'Paul Ashley? What's that? His good deed for the day?'

Ros felt rattled by the tone of his voice and said in Paul's defence, 'I couldn't face clearing the ducks away. He did it for me. He was very kind.'

'Huh! He's paid to be kind. Anyway, do you think it's a good idea having more ducks? You've more than enough to do as it is.'

'We've always had ducks on the farm . . . and they're no trouble. Besides, it will make it easier to tell Mum when I see her later on.'

'Well, you know what's best, I suppose,' Martin concurred, slipping his arm around her waist. 'I was only thinking of you . . . and your mother, when she comes home. After all, you won't be here forever, looking after her, will you?'

Ros slipped out of his encircling arm. Her feelings were in turmoil, what with Jerome's betrayal, her unexpected and foolish liking of Paul and this equally unwanted flirtation with Martin. It was too much to cope with.

'I've no definite plans about that, yet,' she said lightly. 'We'll have to see how Mum gets on. But, for now, new ducks are the way to go!'

It was mid-afternoon before Paul returned with the incubator and Ros set it up, ready for Nick coming home from school. He was a bit later than usual and she wondered if he had missed the school bus. When he did arrive home, he dashed upstairs saying something about sorting out his homework books, so she didn't make an issue of his lateness, especially as he looked less than his normal self. Still upset by the duck debacle, she supposed.

She quickly told him about Paul's idea of trying to incubate some of the ducks' eggs and, after an initial doubting that it would succeed, he took on a more optimistic air and chose a dozen of their most recent duck eggs to place in the incubator.

'It'll be great if some hatch, won't it?' Ros encouraged him. 'And, I tell you what; why don't you tack some fine netting around the lower edges of the duck house to seal off any small gaps? We can't exclude all air holes, but that should prevent another stoat getting in.'

The day which had begun so badly, ended on a positive note at visiting time at the hospital when Eileen announced that the doctors had agreed that she could be discharged the following day as long as someone was available to give her the chance to convalesce.

'I told them I had to be home for my fiftieth birthday in a few weeks time!' Eileen told her with a grin of delight. 'I refuse to spend it lying in bed in hospital!'

Ros was relieved her mum was coming home so soon and, after making a mental note to arrange some sort of party for their mum's half-century, took her leave.

As she neared Melford Green, she could see Joanna Stansbury leading a horse in through the entrance of the riding stables and she tooted lightly on her horn. She hadn't had a chance to speak with her since her return to the village and knew she had a few minutes to spare before going home to bring the herd in from pasture.

A glance in her mirror showed the road was clear behind her and she dropped into second gear with the intention of pulling over on to the other side of the road. To her surprise, however, after a definite glance her way, Joanna averted her gaze and continued towards the stables.

Ros frowned. That was a definite *cut*. Now, what was that about?

With no time to dwell on it further, she drove on into the village. Paul was crossing the village green and, pushing aside Joanna's slight, Ros pulled over to tell him the news of her mother's discharge the following day, knowing that he had intended to visit Eileen again.

'How about transport?' he asked.

Ros indicated the Land Rover with a rueful expression. 'Or I could get a taxi,' she suggested.

'No need for that. I will gladly run you in. It will only mean a little juggling of my schedule. What time shall I pick you up?'

'Oh . . . that's very kind of you, if you're sure. Between ten and half-past?'

'Fine.'

With a few more words about how Nick had reacted to the duck eggs being incubated, they parted company. Ros was surprised to catch sight of her grinning face reflected in the driving mirror. She instantly sobered.

'You can stop that!' she sternly told herself. As Martin had so rightly pointed out, Paul was only doing his job, and her life was in a mess. Paul, and the rest of the villagers, would despise her if they knew the real reason for her being home.

4

The next few days passed uneventfully, with Eileen settling back into life on the farm with the unaccustomed orders to take things easy.

Ros found it difficult enough to keep her mother in bed whilst she made breakfast but, once Nick had gone to school and Ros was down in the cowshed seeing to the milking, Eileen was a law unto herself and was usually busy in the kitchen when Ros came back after taking the dairy herd to pasture.

'I've got to do something!' Eileen protested when Ros bade her sit in the rocking chair with Ginger or Pickle on her knee. 'All I had was a minor heart attack; only a little irregular flutter; a warning, nothing more!'

'And I want to keep it at that!' Ros retorted. 'I tell you what. How about if

I bring the eggs straight up here for you to sort and clean? That would relieve me of a job. We can pack them into boxes in the pantry instead of down in the dairy.'

'And I can still do some baking each day.'

'Not this week!' Ros laughed. 'Every Mothers' Union visitor seems to bring you a dozen scones or a cherry madeira cake!'

'Now, Paul loves a nice fruit cake,' Eileen commented, watching her daughter's face go slightly pink. 'And Martin seems to fancy my 'maids of honour'. Never known such dedicated visitors to a middle-aged lady!'

'Well, it's either you or the cakes!' Ros laughed. 'I'm usually busy elsewhere.'

'Mmm. I have noticed you make yourself scarce when they're around. Playing hard to get, eh? Or is there someone in Paris you've not told me about?'

Ros felt her light-heartedness drain

away. She turned away and busied herself at the sink. 'No,' she said tersely. 'No-one special. I just want to concentrate on keeping things running smoothly here, with no distractions.'

Ros knew she was under close scrutiny by her mother, but didn't want to bring any new anxieties for her to worry about. There were enough closer to home. Nick, for instance. She had found three music CDs under his mattress when she had cleaned his room the previous day. When she had asked him about them he had flushed an angry red and told her it was none of her business . . . which, fair enough, it wasn't . . . except . . .

Now that Mum was home, he seemed to have reverted to his angry-young-man routine, making his aversion to farming quite plain. Even asking his help in planning a surprise fiftieth party for their Mum didn't exactly enthral him, but he did agree to make the invitations on his computer and he did a good job of them. Ros had a quiet word with Paul and he promised to get the Mothers' Union busy on the catering side and said they could use the church hall since the list of those invited seemed to grow by the day.

Problems seemed to follow the family around at the moment, however.

It was only a week or so later when the dogs alerted them to the fact that they had unexpected visitors. They were Ted's younger brother, Kenneth and his younger daughter, Katie-Anne, who was five. Kenneth was a widower, his wife having died of cancer three years earlier.

'Kenneth! What a surprise!' Eileen exclaimed as they entered the kitchen. 'And Katie-Anne! What a big girl you are now!'

Katie-Anne was clutching her doll to her chest with one hand and holding on tightly to her father's trouser leg with the other. She was shying away from the dogs, who had followed them into the kitchen and was obviously distressed by them.

'Take Ben out, Ros,' Eileen said sharply, as Ros appeared in response to the outburst of barking. 'And you, Tiger!' Although the older dog had merely nuzzled his nose towards Katie-Anne's chest. 'The dogs won't hurt you, dear. They only want to say, 'hello'. Sit you down, Ken and I'll make us a brew! Now, you've not come all this way to make sure I'm all right, have you? I told the girls not to worry you! I'm as fit as a fiddle, as you can see!'

Kenneth looked puzzled. He sat down and drew Katie-Anne onto his lap. 'I didn't know you'd been unwell. Nothing serious, I hope.'

'Nothing that time won't put better,' Eileen replied lightly. 'As you can see for yourself. In fact, I've not felt so good for years. So, what have you come for? Not that you're not welcome.'

'Haven't you seen it on the television news?' Ken asked. 'Caroline's gone trekking in Borneo with a friend and they've been reported missing. I'm out of my mind with worry over her.

They've not been heard from for three weeks now, and that's not like her, as you know.'

Caroline, who was almost Ros's age, had set out the previous September to trek around the world after completing her university degree course with first class honours in botanical science.

'No, she's a considerate girl,' Eileen conceded. 'So, what are you intending to do about it?'

'Go out and look for them, of course,' Ken replied. 'Only . . . ' He glanced down at Katie-Anne, who was looking up at him with wide brown eyes, and then across at his sister-in-law, who was pouring some boiling water on top of the tea bags in a brown pot.

'Mmm, I see,' Eileen murmured. It wasn't just a question of having a small child to think about. Being a bit of a wanderlust ran in the Mansell family. That's what had taken her Ted away, the urge to see more of the world, leaving his wife to fend for herself and their family. 'So, when are you thinking of going?'

'Right away! I managed to get a cancellation flight. It departs from Manchester at five to twelve tonight. I thought, that is, I hoped . . . ' He sighed and an expression of defeat flittered across his face. 'You've been ill, you say? I'm sorry. I didn't know. Maybe it's not the best of times to be going, eh?'

Eileen handed him a mug of tea and held out her arms to her niece. 'Come and see what we can find in my cake tin, Katie-Anne. I wouldn't be surprised if there's a nice cake in there with some red cherries in it.'

Katie-Anne obediently slipped off her father's lap and took hold of Eileen's outstretched hand. When she returned to the kitchen she was carrying a plate with a few slices of cake on it. Eileen was close behind with some small plates.

'Put it on that small table, Katie-Anne, and give your daddy one of these plates. I can see you're going to be a big help in the next few weeks. Would you like that, eh? 'Course you'll have to go to school, but I'm sure that will be no problem.'

Kenneth beamed with relief. 'Does that mean . . . ? Oh, I knew I could count on you, Eileen! And Katie-Anne will be as good as gold, won't you, love?'

When Ros came back for her tea-break, she volunteered to make enquiries at the village school. 'In fact you can come with me, Katie-Anne, as soon as we've had our drink . . . and Uncle Ken, too, in case a parental signature is required.'

It was story-time in the infants' class by the time they arrived at the small stone-built school that nestled among a grove of trees next to the church. Katie-Anne willingly joined the other children who were sitting on a carpet around their teacher's feet, while Ros took Kenneth to speak to the headmaster, John Sutton.

He had taught in the school for as

long as Ros could remember, but she managed to parry his questions about her own presence in the village without betraying the real reason. His upper junior class was given the task of silent reading whilst he talked to the two visitors and made arrangement for Katie-Anne to be temporarily enrolled on the school register.

Paul was leaving the church hall on the other side of the church as they passed it on their way back to the farm. Ros introduced him to Ken and Katie-Anne and briefly explained the family situation to him. She noticed a flicker of concern cross his face, but was glad he didn't voice any misgivings he might have. Ken was in enough distress over Caroline, without being made to feel he was putting a burden on Ros and Eileen.

Instead, Paul grasped hold of Ken's shoulder. 'We'll pray for your daughter's safety,' he assured him, 'and I'm sure this young lady will soon have lots of friends to play with. We're a very friendly community here and more than ready to lend a helping hand wherever necessary.'

He turned to look at Ros as he spoke and his eyes lingered on her face as he added, 'Don't forget that, will you, Ros?'

Ros felt a surge of guilt as she met his eyes. Her concealment of the truth from John Sutton had resurrected her awareness of her deception towards everyone else and it seemed as though the intensity of Paul's gaze could see the shadow of guilt in her heart.

'We're fine,' she said brightly, brushing his concern aside. 'And Katie-Anne is going to be a great help, aren't you, love? So, we'd best be getting back. There are eggs to collect and Uncle Ken needs a meal before setting off to the airport.'

'Would it be a help if I take him there?' Paul persisted. 'What time is your flight?'

'No. Like I said, we can manage,' Ros snapped before Ken could answer.

Could he not take 'no' for an answer? She took hold of Katie-Anne's hand. 'Say goodbye to the vicar, Katie-Anne.' And, dragging her behind her, she set off along the road.

Ken was silent for a few minutes as he kept pace with her agitated strides. 'You should have accepted his offer, Ros,' he said mildly, when he sensed she was calming down. 'He seems a nice chap . . . anxious to help.'

'Too anxious, if you ask me!' Ros snapped, knowing she was being unfair. 'You know what it's like in a village. Everyone knowing what everyone else is doing. I've said I'll take you and that's that.'

As it happened, however, Martin phoned to see if Ros would go out for a drink with him and when she gave her reason why not, he said, 'I'll take him.'

Ros immediately felt uncomfortable. 'No. Martin. I can't accept.'

'Why not?'

'Paul offered and I felt irritated and refused. I don't deserve . . . '

'I won't take no for an answer,' Martin replied. 'And put your glad rags on, because you're coming too!' He put the phone down before she could argue.

By the time the evening milking was over and Ros had organised Nick to wash the dishes from their meal, she was too tired to raise any more objections and acquiesced without too much reluctance.

She was also realising how unfair she had been towards Paul and, not wanting to hurt his feelings, hoped that he didn't find out that she had accepted Martin's offer of help after turning down his.

It was the merest mischance that Martin had been given a verbal message from his mother to pass on to Paul, and did so as they passed through the village on the way to the airport. Ros felt like squirming down into her seat and couldn't bear to meet Paul's glance, especially when he smiled warmly at them all and wished them safe travel.

Watching Ros struggle to keep up with the numerous daily farm jobs made Eileen impatient with the progress of her recovery. She longed to be back out there, but knew that the doctor was right in forbidding it.

When she noticed the falling milk yields, she fretted herself even more. Things were slipping. Maybe Hugh Tipton was right and she should think of giving up? Ros couldn't do much more and what a life it was for her. No time to go out and enjoy herself apart from choir practice on Thursday nights and the occasional evening out with Martin. Not even that, this week, with Martin away on a business trip.

Two nice young men, she thought, and both seemed to be sweet on her Ros, but she didn't seem to respond to either in any way that revealed feelings towards them. Young people were much more free and easy with each other in her day, she reflected, but they could still get hurt — and her mother's instinct told her that Ros was hurting in some way.

Just at that moment, Ros was reading a text message on her mobile phone. It was from Jerome Brest, telling her that it was important that she should meet him in Manchester Airport the following day at 4.15 p.m.

5

Ros stared at the message. Why did Jerome suddenly want to see her? He had avoided her when she was still in Paris and made sure she wasn't allowed access to his apartment. So why the change of heart?

A sudden hope sprang within her. Maybe he was going to tell her that he was going to back down? That he was going to tell the truth? But, what was the point in seeing him? Couldn't they discuss whatever it was over the phone?

She brought up his number on the screen and pressed *dial* . . . but there was no response. He either had his phone switched off or he was in an inaccessible place . . . or he was deliberately ignoring her call.

She furiously stabbed out a text message. What is the point? Either say you will tell the truth . . . or I will see you in court!

It was over an hour later when the reply came in. *IMPERATIVE I see you! Please come!*

Ros sighed. She supposed it must be important if he was prepared to fly from Paris to Manchester especially to see her. What had she to lose? A bit of pride and precious loss of time on the farm?

Ros simply told her mother that she was meeting a friend she hadn't seen for a while and Eileen agreed whole-heartedly.

'It'll do you good to get away for a few hours, love. Anyone I know?'

'No, it's someone I met in Paris who is passing through and thought it would be nice to meet up again.'

'Do you miss Paris, Ros? I know you loved it there.' Eileen looked at her daughter anxiously. 'I should be fit enough for you to go back in September. They will keep your job open for you, won't they?'

Ros wondered if it might be a good time to sow a few seeds of preparation of the possibility of her being permanently sacked after the enquiry, but a glance at her mother's anxious expression dissuaded her. It was too soon to risk upsetting her, and it might be needlessly so.

Still, a bit of the outcome might be tentatively mentioned.

'I think I'll be coming back to England,' she said lightly. 'I did love it, but I missed home as well. I'll have to see what turns up.'

'It's not just because of me?'

'No.' That was true, anyway. 'But I would feel a lot happier being within a reasonable distance,' she continued, making herself shrug carelessly. 'There's no need to decide yet. As soon as I decide what to do, I can apply to be reinstated on Shropshire's list and do supply work for a while until something suitable becomes available.

It took all her faith to hold on to that thought the following day when Jerome, after a few banal greetings and light compliments on how well she was looking, ordered two cups of coffee and led her to a small aluminium table. They were seated facing each other when he finally broached the reason for demanding her presence.

'You've got to say that I told you to do the weather checks, but that you forgot,' he said earnestly, taking hold of her hand and running his thumb up and down the inside of her wrist, an action that used to send spirals of pleasure coursing through her. Strangely enough, it no longer did so, she realised analytically. She pulled her mind back to Jerome's words.

'But it isn't the truth,' she reminded him. 'You didn't tell me. All you said was to be at the school gymnasium at eight o'clock to help to check-in the pupils going on the trip.'

'Of course I told you! You've forgotten! Or covering yourself by denying it!' he said sharply. 'You can't face up to being in the wrong, can you?'

Ros tried to pull her hand away, intending to rise from her seat and leave immediately, but Jerome was holding on to her too tightly. Dreading to cause an unpleasant scene, she sank back on to the seat.

'And what about me?' she asked pointedly. 'If I were to take the blame, I'd lose my job! Or doesn't that matter?'

'Well, it's not as important, is it? Besides, you were only brought in at the last minute and without any overall responsibility. No-one would put too much blame on you. They would say it was because of your inexperience. It would blow over in no time. A few years down the line and it will all be forgotten.'

Ros was appalled at his words. 'But two boys drowned in that swollen river, Jerome! Their families want to see justice done. Why should I lie?'

'I could go to prison if I take the blame,' Jerome said flatly. 'My career will be over. Surely your goody-goody attitude to life should enable you to make a slight sacrifice. After all, we did have some good times together, didn't we? I'll stand by you.'

Ros heard the desperation in his voice and her heart was touched, but it would still be lying.

She shook her head and, when she stood up, Jerome let go of her hand. 'It's not fair. You're asking too much,' she said quietly.

'Think about it! Please,' he pleaded. 'There is still a week or so before the enquiry . . . and, if you change your plea and admit liability, it will probably go easier for you.'

Ros looked at him uncertainly. He made it seem as if that were the honourable thing to do, but it would be a deliberate falsehood. 'It doesn't feel right. My family . . . they'd be so disappointed in me.'

'No! They'd be proud of you. You could tell them the truth when it's all over.'

Ros looked up at him sharply. 'So,

you do admit you were to blame, then?'

'Pardon?' Jerome met her gaze but his eyes slid away. 'No, of course not. I'm just looking at it from your point of view,' he blustered. 'I've got a lot of support on my side. His confident smile returned and he spread his hands in a conciliatory way. 'Just promise me you'll think about it, Ros. That's all I ask.'

Ros felt too upset by Jerome's demands to go straight home. She left the airport and was straight into heavy end-of-day traffic that demanded all of her attention, especially since it was now raining quite heavily.

Looking back on their conversation, she couldn't believe he really expected her to take the blame for his negligence and decided to waste no more time worrying about it.

Reassured by this decision, she glanced at her watch, surprised at how time had flown. It would be too late for choir practice when she got back into Melford Green, but she could attend the meeting about the youth club that was scheduled to be held later at the vicarage.

As she parked the Land Rover, the choir practice was just finishing and Ros fell into step with some of the choir who wished to attend the meeting as they hurried across the car park towards the vicarage with a variety of umbrellas sheltering them from the worst of the rain.

There was no formality about waiting until Paul was ready to join them. His housekeeper had left a small table ready in the lounge with tea, coffee and biscuits and Bill Metcalf, one of the Parish Church Council members offered to 'be mother' and pour out for everyone.

Ros accepted a cup of coffee and a chocolate biscuit and drifted across the room to where she had spotted Joanna Stansbury, still not having met her face-to-face since her return from France.

'Hi, Joanna! Long time no see!' she

said in greeting. 'How's the riding school going?'

She was totally unprepared for the look of scorn on Joanna's face when she turned to face her.

'Oh, it's you!' Joanna said ungraciously. 'What do you want?'

Ros had in mind to make tentative enquiries about the possibility of Katie-Anne having riding lessons but was completely put off stroke by Joanna's open hostility.

She took an involuntary step backwards, aware that her hand was shaking and her cup of coffee in danger of being spilled. She swallowed hard. 'Do you have a problem with me over something, Joanna?'

'I should think it's you who had the problem,' Joanna said coldly. 'Just how many men do you need to keep you happy? Or is this the way it's done in France these days?'

Ros blinked. 'Pardon?'

'Oh, don't pretend you don't know what I'm taking about! We saw you, holding hands across a table with some man at the airport!'

'At the airport?' Ros echoed. 'Today? I didn't see you there.'

'Well, you wouldn't, would you? You only had eyes for each other. You've no right to come back with your flighty French ways. So, stop fluttering your eyes at people in this village and pushing in where you've no right to be.'

Ros realised that the room had fallen silent and her face, that had felt drained of colour, suddenly flushed with heat. She knew people must have overheard Joanna's words and wanted to put matters straight, but when she opened her mouth to speak, no sound came out. Besides, what could she say? She didn't want to have to explain about Jerome, and it was no-one else's business, anyway.

And who did Joanna mean? Who was she accusing her of fluttering her eyelashes at? Paul? Had her liking of him been so obvious? The thought flitted across her mind that Joanna must have a liking for him also. Was she warning her to keep away from him?

She opened her mouth to say that that was as much up to Paul as herself, only to be preceded by Paul's voice behind her saying, 'Shall we bring the meeting together, ladies and gentlemen? We have a lot to discuss.'

Ros's heart sank and she was aware that her face had again flamed with heat. Had Paul heard what Joanna had said? Did he realise that he was the subject of the strained atmosphere? There was no way of knowing and Ros carefully avoided making eye contact with him.

Thankfully, Paul's presence broke the tension and everyone resumed chattering again as they made their way to the assortment of seating that was placed in the room. Ros was aware of a few wry or sympathetic glances sent her way but no-one made any comment about the brief exchange . . . not in Ros's hearing, anyway, though she was sure there would be comments made when neither she nor Joanna were present.

She carefully chose to sit as far away from Joanna as she could and also distance herself from Paul. She tried to push the incident from her mind but it would be untrue to say that it didn't keep intruding.

She demurred when asked to be willing to stand as a proposed member of the committee and also declined to be placed in any position of responsibility covering any activities that might be planned, giving her own uncertain future plans as the deterrent. She did, however, let her name be added to the list of volunteers willing to be put on a roster for being on duty on Youth Club evenings.

Privately, she knew she had disappointed Paul and could only shake her head when one of the others present pointed out that as a qualified teacher, she already had the authorisation and expertise.

Joanna earned Brownie Points by offering cut-rate riding lessons for club members and Martin, a latecomer to the meeting, offered to raise sponsorship for the club among his various business contacts. The Mothers' Union had already offered to run a tuck shop and other refreshments on club nights.

It was after half-past ten when Paul brought the meeting to a close, thanking everyone for their time and support, promising to have the first month's roster ready for Sunday.

Ros was anxious to get home. She murmured a few 'goodnights' and slipped through the departing attendees without being confronted by Joanna or Paul, feeling that she could not have coped with either of them at that point in the proceedings.

Hovering in the manse doorway, wondering whether to put her coat over her head or simply make a dash through the rain, she was briefly detained by Martin, who seemed keen to share that he had had a successful business trip and would she care to go home with him for a drink or two?

Ros felt tired and the beginning of a headache seemed to be lurking around the eyes. 'I'm sorry, Martin, it's been a long day. D'you mind if I say no?'

'That's OK. How about a meal tomorrow evening? Our last Friday night free of responsibility,' he quipped.

It seemed easier to accept the invitation than to make a string of excuses in refusal, and Ros was thankful to escape outside to the Land Rover and drive the short distance home to her bed and privacy from curious speculation.

The downstairs light was on, but it was obvious that her mother had gone to bed, for which Ros was thankful. She didn't feel up to launching into any explanations about how her meeting with her *friend* had gone, nor about the meeting at church. A note was propped up against a jug on the kitchen table.

Ros read it. It was from her mother, asking if she would stay up until Nick arrived home as he wasn't in yet and the last bus had long since passed through the village.

It wasn't as though Nick didn't have a key. He did. But she knew their mother didn't want the fifteen-year-old boy to think he could come in at any time he liked without someone being there to monitor his homecoming.

Ros felt exasperated by her brother. Didn't he realise that their mother could do without any extra undue cause of worry?

She heard a car door slam and the sound of their dogs barking and she crossed the kitchen to peer out into the yard. Ben was fastened on a long chain that was just long enough to allow him to reach almost to the farm gate to deter any intruders. From the brevity of their barking, Ros gathered that the latecomer was her brother.

She was right.

Nick almost fell into the kitchen in his haste to get out of the wet and pulled up abruptly when he saw Ros. His face fell.

'Oh! I didn't expect . . . That is, you

shouldn't have waited up for me.'

'No, maybe not!' Ros snapped. 'Where on earth have you been until this hour? It's past eleven — and where have you got that jacket from? It's not yours!'

Her final remark gave Nick the excuse to break eye contact and look down. 'This?

'Oh, it's . . . er . . . Gary's. He . . . er . . . lent it to me . . . because of the rain. His brother drove me home.'

'Isn't he the one who's been in a lot of trouble with the police? You don't go out with him, do you?'

'Not often. Anyway, if the inquisition's over, I'm off to bed. See you in the morning, eh?'

Ros still felt slightly uneasy about Nick and his friends but, short of getting their mother to lay down the law a bit more, there wasn't much she could do about it right now. She sighed, knowing that what he needed was a father's guiding hand . . . and that was out of her control.

6

Ros was disappointed on both counts. For some reason, Ben started barking again but when she slipped into her dressing-gown and slippers and went down to the kitchen to peer through the window into the farm yard, Ben had quietened by then and apart from the fact that it was still raining, there was no sign of anything untoward.

Ros found her mind continually going over the two unpleasant incidents of the previous day. She would have normally shrugged off the incident with Joanna as being no more than petty jealousy on the other girl's part, but it came too close on the heels of Jerome's latest input into the fatal accident at her French school for her to dismiss it so readily.

She wished she hadn't come home and that the village acquired a new vicar in her absence. The depth of her disquiet made her realise that she was beginning to like Paul more than she had originally thought possible.

Not that she was intending to fall in love with him or anything stupid like that. As for Joanna, maybe it was a bit of wishful thinking on Joanna's part? She wouldn't be the first female to cast her eyes in the direction of a young, handsome vicar.

The following day, she awakened just before seven o'clock and rolled out of bed with a groan. She normally had the cows in from pasture by now and, from the quietness of the yard, she knew that Nick hadn't risen early to do it for her.

She banged on Nick's door as she passed and bade him get up and help her, hastily poured herself a glass of milk from the fridge and buttered a slice of bread. Hurriedly swallowing both, she opened the door into the outer porch.

She dragged on her Wellingtons and an old water-proof jacket and set off across the yard towards the pasture gate. Something, she wasn't sure what, made her glance over her shoulder in the opposite direction, towards the stream that usually babbled its way down the length of the farmyard, wending its way through the fields beyond.

The whole right-hand side of the farmyard was awash and the banks of the stream were completely submerged under at least a foot of water!

She turned and ran across the yard, only slowing down when the water was half-way up her Wellingtons and she became unsure of her foothold on the slippery underwater surface. She couldn't tell where the stream had burst its bank and went warily in case she suddenly slipped down into the swirling water.

To her dismay, she suddenly realised that some of the hens were out of their cabins. Most of them were sheltering in the large barns, but as she made her way down the yard towards the far end, she could see what looked like a bundle of white rags caught up in the swollen stream, lodged against what seemed to be a barrier of fallen tree branches and other woodland debris. She couldn't get near enough to reach it, but knew without doubt that at least one hen had got caught in the overflowing water and had drowned.

'Ros! Wait! I'm coming!' Nick's voice called. 'What happened? How did the stream get blocked like that?'

Ros helplessly shook her head. 'I don't know. Branches must have fallen off some trees and got washed down as the water-level rose.'

With Nick holding on to her, Ros edged nearer until she could grasp the end of a particularly large branch and she began to pull at it, though without too much success.

'My feet feel secure, Nick. If you carefully edge yourself forward until you can grab hold of it, we might be able to shift it together.'

Nick did as she suggested and they

managed to partially dislodge the branch, allowing some of the smaller debris to be whirled away in the fast-flowing current. It was enough to stop the water rising any higher and Ros was sure the level was dropping slightly.

'Go and fetch the cows in, Nick, and I'll start setting up in the milking shed. We'll leave this for now and I'll sort it out later. I might have to get some help.'

Nick did as he was bidden and they were halfway through the milking when Hugh put in his appearance, complaining that their stream had flooded his land, which bordered theirs just beyond the far bank.

'It's ruined my vegetable patch,' he grumbled, 'and I'll be seeking compensation. Bad management, that's what it is. You should have anticipated a flood like this and cleared the land the other side of the bridge. If your ma had let me have half the stream, like I've been asking for years, I'd have seen to it, and this wouldn't have happened.'

'I didn't know the land needed clearing. Why didn't you say, if you knew it needed doing? We'd have got it done somehow.'

'None of my business, see! Maybe now you'll realise you've taken on too much.'

'Farming is always hard work, Hugh. We've just got to get on with it, like everyone else.' She turned to her brother. 'Go and get ready for school, now, Nick . . . and, if you see Mum, tell her as gently as you can what has happened and assure her it's under control. Take over from Nick, Hugh, if you will. I want to get finished as soon as we can.'

By the time the milking was done, the cows returned to pasture and the milking parlour swilled clean, Ros was ready for a break and returned to the farmhouse. The aroma of frying bacon greeted her. Eileen was up and dressed and had telephoned a neighbour who had a child of similar age to Katie-Anne and asked if she would stop on her way past the farm and pick up Katie-Anne to take her to school.

Ros tucked in to a tasty breakfast with no second bidding. As she ate, she repeated what Hugh had said to her about the non-clearance of the wooded land just over the road bridge.

Eileen shook her head. 'I know I've been out of commission for a week or two, love, but there was no debris to speak of lying over there. I hired two men after the winter storms so it's not that long since it was cleared. It must have come from higher up, and that's out of our jurisdiction. There must have been a cloudburst somewhere. At least it's stopped raining now. Is the level going down?'

'Yes, and I'd better get back out there to see what needs doing. Once the water has left the yard I'll let the rest of the hens out, but I'll leave collecting the eggs until later.'

'I'll see to the hens, love. I feel fit enough.'

Eileen looked pleased to be allowed to resume one of her morning tasks and, knowing it would be fruitless to argue the point, Ros agreed.

She hadn't been long back at the debris blocking the stream when the dogs began to bark and rushed up the yard. She heard a vehicle drive into the yard, followed by a familiar voice calling her name. It was Paul.

She let go of the branch she was trying to haul out of the stream and eased her back straight, aware of a frisson of pleasure coursing through her as she watched Paul striding down the yard towards her, ploughing through the water as though it weren't there.

'Hi! Have you called to see Mum? She's in the dairy sorting the eggs,' she greeted him.

Paul smiled. 'No, I came to see you. To see if I could lend a hand.' He indicated his attire. 'I'm dressed for the job, as you can see.'

'How did you know? Don't say Hugh

has been beating the jungle drums again?'

Paul laughed. 'No, it was Katie-Anne. I take the early morning assembly in school on Fridays and when I asked if anyone knew of any needs for prayer, her hand shot up and said her Auntie Ros was in great need.'

Ros could quite imagine that Katie-Anne would have given a lively description of the flooding, and she welcomed the extra pair of hands that were being offered.

Turning her mind away from just whose hands they were, she told Paul what she was trying to do. He carefully joined her in the swirling cold water and, together, they attacked the pile of debris that was still caught fast, tugging at whatever seemed likely to come free.

Success came suddenly, as they both tugged at a particular piece. It seemed to leap out of the blockage, taking them both by surprise and, as the released water surged forward, it swept them both off their feet. They tumbled back against the sodden banking, chest high in the water. Ros felt Paul grasp her in his arms as they fell.

The force of the water turned her over and would have possibly tumbled her farther downstream if Paul hadn't held her tightly. Before Ros knew what had happened, she was lying face down on top of Paul with his arms still clasped around her.

'Oh!'

Her surprised gasp was stilled as a further thrust of water and debris tumbled them both over again and they halted with Paul lying on top of Ros. He scrabbled with his feet to obtain a firm foothold and pressed his elbows into the soft bank.

Their eyes held for what seemed to be an age and Ros could feel his breath upon her face, though it was no more than seconds before Paul pressed his lips against hers. The chill of the water lost all meaning as Ros responded to his kiss.

When he lifted his head and smiled

into her eyes, Ros smiled back.

'That was unexpected!' Paul said with an element of surprise in his voice. 'I'm sorry! I don't usually kiss helpless maidens in distress! I hope I haven't offended you?'

'N . . . no. I . . . I think it was the stress of the moment,' she stammered. 'I suppose we could have been swept away and drowned, but we weren't . . . and we . . . '

' . . . were light-headed with relief,' Paul suggested, beginning to raise himself to his feet, still smiling at her. He held out his hand to her. 'Here, let me help you up.'

He laughed self-consciously as he helped her to scramble up the bank and on to the firmer ground of the farmyard. 'I suppose instead of kissing you, I should have been giving thanks to God . . . though I'm sure He understands.'

'Huh, with all that's been happening to me in the past few months, I don't think God likes me any more,' Ros said, aware that she was probably shocking Paul, but felt unable to keep her thoughts unspoken.

Paul held her away from him and looked directly into her eyes. 'I know something is worrying you, Ros,' he said gently. 'Maybe, at some point, you'll feel able to share some of it with me. If you do, it will be in strictest confidence. But, whatever, even though I don't know the cause of your problems, I do know it's not because God doesn't like you. Haven't you been listening Sunday by Sunday? He loves you!'

'Hey! You there! Ros Mansell!'

The angry shout rang across the farmyard and Ros turned to see Joanna Stansbury striding towards them, her face glowering.

Ros guiltily slipped out of the circle of Paul's comforting arms and faced Joanna. 'Look, I'm sorry, Joanna!' she began to apologise, though why she felt it necessary, she wasn't quite sure. 'We're soaking wet and . . . '

'Huh! So you already know about it, do you?' Joanna stormed, ignoring both their appearance and Ros's attempts to divert her wrath to a later occasion. 'It's downright disgraceful and you needn't think I'm going to pay next month's rent until it's all sorted. The horses could have been killed or badly injured for all you care. It's lucky for you that Mr Williamson was driving slowly because of the wet roads and was able to pull up in time!'

Ros shook her head, her brain completely bemused. 'Pardon? I don't know what you're talking about. What has that got to do with me?'

'Look, Joanna,' Paul began, but Joanna took no heed to his attempted intervention.

'My horses in the top paddock got out through a gap in the hedge and were loose on the road twenty minutes after I'd let them out this morning. You know very well that it's your responsibility to see that the hedges are kept in good order. I'll be claiming compensation for any extra feeding costs until they can graze safely in the paddock again and you can count yourself lucky to be getting off so lightly!'

Ros briefly closed her eyes. Two claims for compensation in less than three hours. What had Paul said about not being tested beyond what you are able to cope with? She took a deep breath.

'I'm sorry, Joanna. I didn't know the hedges were damaged. I haven't had time to look over them,' she added lamely, knowing that Joanna was right. It was their responsibility to keep the hedges in order.

'Hmm, well, I hope you'll make it your priority to mend the gap and check the rest,' Joanna said, somewhat mollified by Ros's low-key reaction. 'If you ask me, you're in this way above your head, Ros. Don't you think so, Paul?' she added, smiling up at him and suddenly becoming aware of the state of his clothes. 'Why! You're soaking

105

wet!' She turned and looked at Ros. 'And you are, too! What have you been up to?'

'An untimely swim!' Paul said with an attempt at humour. 'Look, Joanna. As you can see, neither Ros nor I are in a fit state to stand and talk. I'm sure Ros is sympathetic to your grievance and will discuss it with you later. Right, Ros?'

Ros nodded in agreement.

'So, if you'll let me go home and get changed, I'll come round to your riding stables and I'll take a look at the damaged hedge for you. I'm sure Ros has plenty of other things to be getting on with this morning.'

Suddenly, she was fully aware of how wet and cold she was and couldn't prevent a violent shiver running through her. Paul took hold of her arm and began to lead the way towards the farmhouse. As they drew level with the dairy, Eileen appeared in the doorway.

'Hello there, I thought I heard voices. Oh, my goodness! Have you both been in the stream? Let's get you out of those wet clothes and into something dry.'

Paul held up his hand. 'Thank you, Eileen, but it's as quick for me to go home. Ros will tell you what happened. At least we've cleared the stream so there shouldn't be any more problems there. I'll see you later, Ros . . . and you, Joanna. Just give me half-an-hour.'

'I'm in the Land Rover. I'll give you a lift,' Ros heard Joanna offer as they departed.

Ros smiled wryly, remembering Paul's kiss. If this were a contest, would that be *round one* to her?

Was Joanna aiming to win the next round?

7

Paul didn't return that day. He telephoned to say that an elderly parishioner was dying and he had been called to her bedside. When he offered to come later that evening, Eileen gave Ros's apologies and said that she was going for a meal with Martin.

Ros was unsure of her reaction. She had enjoyed his kiss, but felt too unsettled in others area of her life to want to seriously pursue any sort of relationship . . . and she sensed that a relationship with Paul would be serious. Was she ready? She would rather get the forthcoming enquiry out of the way first.

Martin was different. Although he paid attention to her, she sensed it was merely mild flirting on his part, and that was fine by her.

He picked her up just after half-past

seven and drove to a village pub he knew on the outskirts of Shrewsbury. Not surprisingly, he already knew of the flooded stream and the damaged hedge at the riding school and offered concern and sympathy when she told him that both Hugh and Joanna were threatening to sue for compensation.

'That's a bit tough, especially on top of the hassle and everything,' he agreed, 'but I suppose you can't blame them. Looking after your boundaries is a land-owner's prime concern. Dad sends our estate manager round our boundary every week to check that it's in good order. I'll ask him to let me know if there's any wear and tear on our adjoining boundary, shall I? Talking of which . . . '

He paused for a moment, picked up his glass of wine, swirled it around and seemed to look at it intently before taking a sip.

'Go on,' Ros urged.

Martin looked a bit uncomfortable. 'I know I've said it before and you rejected it out of hand, but I do really think you have taken on more than you can manage, Ros . . . and it isn't going to get any easier. The first silage crop will be ready soon and if you're keeping many acres for winter hay, you'll have all that to see to as well. You'll have to get in extra help, which, if rumours are to be believed, the farm budget can't stand it.'

Ros felt acutely embarrassed, even though she knew that every word he had said was true.

'I really don't think it's any of your business!' she said sharply. 'If that's the reason you've brought me out here . . . to . . . to tell me I'm making a hopeless mess of the farm, then . . . '

Martin laid his hand over hers. 'I'm not saying that. I know you're doing the best you can, but it's not enough. The farm was failing long before your mother's heart attack. It's been obvious to everyone that she couldn't manage to farm on her own either — no-one could. You've either to hire help — or . . . '

110

' . . . go under?'

'I wasn't going to say that. Neither you nor your mother is the sort to *go under*! No, I was going to say, *or sell*.'

'Sell? It would break Mum's heart. Her family have had the farm for generations and there's always been a son or a daughter to take it on.'

'And who is it going to be in your generation? Debbie? She's already married to a publican. Nick, who is loudly proclaiming to anyone who is listening that he doesn't want to be a farmer? Or yourself, a teacher? You're going to have to face it sooner or later, Ros . . . and I don't want to see you get hurt.'

Ros had listened in silence. Now she raised anguished eyes to meet his 'It's Mum I don't want to see get hurt,' she said quietly. 'She's getting back on her feet, now. She saw to the eggs today. Once she's up and running again, we'll manage. Nick will help in the school holidays. Hugh Tipton helps out with the milking . . . and he's another one who is always telling me we ought to sell! Some of it to him, of course.'

'Oh, I wouldn't do that! He'll offer rock bottom price. And anyway, you won't have to sell it all. Just reduce it to a manageable size.'

'We could hire land out,' Ros said thoughtfully. 'That would bring in some income, wouldn't it?'

'I'd agree . . . if either you or Nick were going to want to take on the farm. As it is . . . '

'We're not,' Ros agreed flatly.

'So? What are your options?'

'I won't say it. I can't.'

'It needn't be all of it. Think about it. Talk it over with Eileen . . . and, if it's any help to you in making a decision, my father is willing to buy most of the acreage that borders our land.'

Ros snatched her hand away from Martin's comforting caressing. Her face flooded with anger. 'So, that's what this is all about, is it? You're joining the vultures waiting to swoop down on us. Well, you can tell your father the answer is no.' She wiped her lips with her napkin and stood up. 'I think it's time to take me home, Martin!'

Martin stood up also. 'As you wish, but let me just say, he would offer the current market price — or above. He isn't out to cheat you.'

Ros looked at him coldly. 'I don't want to hear any more. Take me home!'

It was an uncomfortable ride home. Martin attempted to make light conversation, but Ros felt too upset to respond. When they reached their gate, she bade him 'goodnight' in clipped tones and got out of the car.

Eileen was still downstairs but admitted that she was about to go to bed. 'I didn't expect you home quite so early, love. Everything all right, is it?'

Ros wondered whether to lie and say everything was fine, but it wasn't. On the other hand, she was too upset to hold a calm and logical discussion right there and then ... and her mother looked tired.

'Not really,' she admitted, 'but it can wait. Is Nick in?'

'Not yet, but don't worry. You have an early night. You've been working hard, love. Don't think I don't realise it. I'll leave a note reminding him to lock the door. It'll be all right, for once.'

With that, they bade each other 'goodnight' and went to bed.

Ros tossed and turned, wondering why everything in her life had turned topsy-turvy in the past few months. Deep down, she knew that much of what Martin had said made economical sense but she didn't want to face it.

And their dad. Old resentments surfaced. If he hadn't upped and gone, none of this would be happening. They'd be managing fine. Her mother wouldn't have worked herself into the ground and there'd have been no heart attack.

A vision of Paul's face came to her mind and she thought of his words about not being tested beyond what she was able to bear. How did that verse continue? She searched her memory. Wasn't it something like, 'there will be a way of escape so that you are able to bear it?'

Was selling their 'way of escape'? But, wasn't that giving in? Being defeatist? And what about the rest of her problems? The enquiry? Her teaching career might be over. What would she do, then? She might be glad of the farm, if that came about.

The following day, as soon as milking was over, Ros organised Nick to start on the hens. 'And let Katie-Anne help you,' she suggested. 'She'll be very careful, won't you, Katie-Anne?'

'Yes. Auntie Eileen has given me a special basket. I'll be able to tell daddy about it when he rings again. won't I? D'you think he's found Caroline yet?'

'He might have. He said there are no public phones where he is and his mobile might have lost its battery charge. We've got to keep praying.'

'He's looking for Caroline like I'm looking for eggs. Its exciting when I find an egg and I'll be excited when daddy finds Caroline!'

'We all will, love!'

Ros left Nick and Katie-Anne to search out the hen's favourite nesting places, while she tried to pull the debris from the stream further away in case they had more rain later. She had almost finished when she saw that Paul had arrived again. She blushed, remembering the pleasure of his kiss and hoped he would think it was because of her exertions with the awkwardly-shaped debris.

'Hello, Ros! Eileen said you were down here. How're things today?' he said with a smile, his voice warm with . . . was it affection? Or did he greet all his parishioners that way?

Ros noticed how his eyes crinkled at the corners when he smiled and the colour of them darkened. She felt quite fascinated by their intensity and had to blink suddenly in order to tear her gaze away.

'F . . . fine,' she said quickly, to cover up her delay in speaking. 'As you can see, I have nearly cleared this lot. I'm going to drag it over to the wood pile and sort it out later.'

'I'm glad it's still here. Where's that large branch that caused our ducking yesterday?'

Ros was puzzled. 'Just over there,' she indicated behind her. 'Why?'

'Just something I want to check . . . something I noticed when I was looking at the broken hedge at Joanna's yesterday.'

Huh! So he had found time to go there yesterday! She was surprised at the surge of jealousy she felt and silently condemned herself for it. He'd said he would go, hadn't he?

'Yes! Just as I thought! Look!'

Paul dragged at the branch and pointed to its cut end. Ros stared at it.

'It's been cut with a saw!' she exclaimed.

'Yes, just like the hedge at the riding school! And, if you think about the size of this piece, how did it get washed under the bridge? With the water-level as high as it was yesterday, it should have got jammed there! There's no way it came through and got carried this far down. And, even if it had somehow been swept under the bridge, it would have lodged itself higher up the yard, over there.'

Paul pointed to where the stream curved past a brick-built section of the bank where, years ago, her father, Ted Mansell, had constructed some steps down into the stream. They used the place to gain access to the stream to wash out the feeding trays and suchlike.

Ros realised what Paul was implying. 'You mean, someone deliberately cut the branch and made sure it stuck in the stream just here where it would cause most damage. Any higher up and the water could have found a way around it without flooding the farm-yard. But, who would do that?'

Paul made a wry expression and shrugged his shoulders. 'I don't know. Someone who wants to cause you some hardship, make you discouraged? I'd hate to think it was anyone local, someone we know. How secure is the farmyard at night?'

'The gate is barred, but it could be undone. With Katie-Anne being a bit fearful of the dogs, Ben is chained but ... ' She paused, remembering being disturbed the night before last. 'Now that I think of it, I did hear him barking on Thursday night. I went downstairs and looked out of the window, but couldn't see anything amiss. I assumed he had been spooked by the storm. He didn't bark for long, though.' She pursed her lips thoughtfully. 'Maybe that was because he knew the intruder? But, who would do such a thing?'

Suddenly, she remembered what Martin had said last night. His father wanted to buy some of their land . . . or, was 'willing to purchase some', as if he were doing them a favour.

'Martin Felton!' she said out loud.

'Pardon?'

'Martin Felton! He told me last night that his father wanted to buy some of our land . . . the fields that share their boundary with ours. The rotter! No doubt he was trying to sweet-talk me into persuading Mum to sell land to them . . . and making things difficult at the same time. Well, he won't get away with it.'

Ros felt furious. How could she have been so gullible? He'd been laughing up his sleeve at her, whilst pretending friendship!

'I must say, that surprises me,' Paul was saying. 'I know Geoffrey Felton likes to play the 'lord of the manor' a bit, but I don't think he'd stoop to criminal acts of vandalism. He's my Church Warden!'

'Maybe he knows nothing about it. Martin might have taken that role on himself. All his father would know was the end result. Well, he has another think coming! I'm going right round there this instant.'

'Ros, don't jump to hasty conclusions,' Paul warned, laying his hand on her arm. 'Let's consider this carefully before you rush off.'

'I really don't see what there is to consider,' Ros objected. 'It's blatantly obvious that he's the one responsible. Had it all timed to a nicety, didn't he, knowing he was taking me out for a meal and could slip his offer in while I was still reeling. What a fool he must think me!'

Paul gently held her in his arms and stroked down her hair. 'Don't be too hard on yourself, Ros.' He drew back and tilted up her chin. 'You're upset, and rightly so, but promise me you'll give yourself time to think it over before you rush round there.'

His eyes were serious and full of concern for her. Ros felt herself being comforted by his presence. 'I'll not go round today,' she eventually promised.

'And not on the Lord's Day?'

She managed a short laugh. 'On Monday, then,' she conceded. 'I'll wait until then.'

8

Paul helped Ros take the large pieces of debris to the woodpile and then suggested that, while she finished the task on her own, he could take Nick with him to mend the hedge at the riding school.

'Are you sure you have the time?' Ros enquired.

'I always allow myself some time for personal activities on Saturdays.' Paul assured her. 'Sometimes I go to a football match . . . but, today, I fancy some outdoor life, so what better than layering a hedge?'

'And there was me thinking vicars only worked on Sundays!' Ros teased.

'In your dreams!' Paul laughed. 'Sometimes I'm lucky to get Saturday afternoon free. Anyway, young Nick, how about it?'

'Yeh, I suppose so. How come you

know about layering hedges?'

'My father manages a large country estate in Cheshire,' Paul told him, as they set off up the field. 'I've often worked alongside him. Quite enjoyed it, too, but I knew it wasn't what I wanted to do for the rest of my life.'

'Huh! Heard God telling you to be a vicar, did you?' Nick asked somewhat scathingly.

Paul didn't appear to take offence. 'Yes, as a matter of fact, I did. A very clear call . . . and I've never regretted responding as I did.'

'Didn't your dad mind?'

'Yes, he did. Very much so. He tried all he could to make me change my mind.'

'Was your dad angry?'

Paul nodded. 'At first, but I always helped out in my holidays and worked hard at my chosen career. He came round eventually. We're good friends again, now.'

'Hmm!' Nick hesitated, then said, 'I miss my dad, you know.'

Paul nodded again. 'Yes, I expect you do. D'you never hear from him?'

'Not for a while. I reckon he's forgotten all about us by now.'

'Probably not. Fathers don't usually forget their children.'

'Then why doesn't he come home? Everything would be all right if Dad were here!' Nick said, kicking at the ground.

'I don't know the answer to that, Nick. I wish I did. Maybe he'd like to, but doesn't know how. Would you forgive him, if he came home?'

Nick looked surprised at the question. 'Forgive him? I suppose so. I'd ask him why he went, and why he stayed away so long, but I'd be glad to see him back.'

Paul glanced at him appraisingly. 'That's a mature attitude, Nick. I think your dad would be proud of you.'

Nick felt pleased but didn't want to appear so. 'That doesn't help us manage without him, though, does it?'

'No, but it might help you cope with

the situation as it is. What do you want to do for a career, by the way?'

'I don't know . . . anything but farming!'

'Well, you've got two years yet before you leave school. That's plenty of time to decide what you want to do. And I think your dad would understand you not wanting to be a farmer. After all, he ran away from farming, didn't he?'

'You mean, not away from us kids?'

'No. Didn't you realise? Your mother has told me, your dad never wanted to farm. He thought he could make a go of it, but it wasn't in his blood, just like it's not in yours.'

Nick was silent for a few minutes, then he said, 'I thought I'd leave school this summer. There's no point staying on. Mum wants me to go to agricultural college, but I've said no.'

'Then, why leave school? You'll end up in a dead-end job and it will be harder to get back into education later. Stick at it. There are all sorts of courses you can do at Sixth Form College.'

Ros cleared all the remnants of the debris from the bank of the stream, checked that the eggs were finished and then took Katie-Anne back to the farmhouse, where Eileen was busy baking some scones.

'Go and wash your hands and then come and help me with this baking, Katie-Anne,' Eileen invited, 'and there's a letter from France on the sideboard for you, Ros.'

Ros's stomach lurched. She could see at a glance that it was official. 'It's from my school,' she managed to say quite casually, although her heart was racing. She slipped it onto the back pocket of her jeans. 'I'm ready for a cup of coffee, Mum. Shall I put the kettle on?'

'Yes, and the first batch of biscuits are cooling. Pop a few on to a plate, there's a dear. Aren't you going to read it, then?'

Ros knew it was no good putting it off. And she knew what it would say. Even so, the closeness of the date made her mind reel. 'Oh, no!' She couldn't help it. The words came out before she had time to stop them.

'Bad news, is it, Ros? They don't want you back, do they? I thought you could stay until the end of term, and beyond, if you wish.'

The dismay in Eileen's voice didn't make it any easier for Ros. 'They want me there on Monday, for a meeting,' she added hastily. 'Some . . . er . . . sorting out to do. They've sent me a flight ticket for Sunday evening and booked me in a B&B for three nights. I should be back on Wednesday . . . in good time for your birthday.'

'I hope so, love. Still, we're only going out for a nice meal somewhere. We could always choose another night, couldn't we?' Eileen hastily wiped her hands on a cloth and went over to the phone. 'I'd better see who I can get to come in and help me while you're away. I'm sure Claire's mother will pick Katie-Anne up and take her to school. Will Hugh give me extra hours, I wonder? I can't ask Nick. His GCSEs start soon. Oh, dear.'

Ros felt terrible. 'I'll tell them I can't go,' she said impulsively. 'They'll have to fix another date.'

'Can they do that, love? No, there's no point! It'll be difficult to fit in whenever it is. Once all that rain has drained away, we've to start on the first crop of silage. No, best get this visit over with while the ground is too soft for the tractor.'

Ten minutes on the phone brought a less than satisfactory response. 'Claire's mother will take Katie-Anne to school but, as you probably gathered, Hugh can't oblige. His back's bad. Might be better, he said, but not to count on him. He spent most of the time saying, 'I told you you couldn't manage. And none of the nearby farmers were too keen on making a promise either. They're watching the weather to do their own first cutting.'

Eileen sank down in a chair, causing Ros a start of alarm but her mother shook her head at her concern. 'I'm all right, love. Just dispirited, really.' She raised her head and looked steadily at Ros. 'It looks like it's the end of an era, doesn't it?'

'Don't say that, Mum! We'll manage. Just delay the silage crop until I get back. It's only four days or so. We'll get someone to help. I'll change the beds and hoover upstairs before lunch,' she offered, wanting to leave as few jobs as possible for her mother to do while she was away. 'Would you like to help me with the dusting, Katie-Anne?'

She worked swiftly, anxious to get the job finished. Nick's room was the last one to do. As usual, many of his clothes were discarded on to the floor.

'Why is Nick's room such a mess?' Katie-Anne asked.

'That's boys for you, I'm afraid!' Ros commented as she bent down to pick up the jacket she had seen him wearing the other night, tut-tutting at his careless treatment of someone else's property. 'That's strange!'

She had noticed that a metal security

tab was still firmly fixed in the lining. 'Now, how did that get past the security shield in the shop?'

Her spirit sank as she spoke her thoughts aloud, realising the jacket hadn't been purchased. Nick must have stolen it. She remembered the CDs she had found a few weeks ago and she slipped her hand under his mattress. Yes, they were still there. She rocked back on her heels, wondering what should she do. Laying the coat on the end of Nick's bed, she decided she would have to hear what he had to say before taking it any further.

When they returned to the kitchen, Nick and Paul had returned and were enjoying a mug of coffee and some crunchy oat biscuits. Eileen had broken the news of Ros's impending brief return to France and was just turning down Nick's predictable offer to stay off school, but Paul's offer to help was gratefully accepted.

When Ros accompanied him to the farm gate, he gently took hold of both of her shoulders and looked at her in some concern.

'I realise it must be important for you to make this trip to France just before Eileen's birthday, or you wouldn't be going,' he said quietly. 'Is it anything I can help you with? You know I would do anything in my power to help you, even if it's only a shoulder to lean on.'

Ros raised her troubled eyes but shook her head. How she wished she could unburden herself to him. She longed to be able to simply lean against him and feel his strength support her . . . but she knew, if she started to speak of it, she would burst into tears and utterly disgrace herself — and she needed to talk to Nick in an attempt to sort out his problems before he got into serious trouble. Besides, what would Paul think of them? What a family of trouble!

So, she shook her head numbly, choking back the threatening tears. 'No, it's nothing,' she managed to mumble. 'It'll be all right!'

'I hope so,' he said tenderly. 'And, if not, you know where I am, at any time, night or day. At least the Mothers' Union ladies have got your mother's surprise party in hand for Saturday, so we'll be all right there . . . and, no arguments, I'll take you to the airport on Sunday afternoon.'

Ros nodded, unable to speak. She turned away and ran back to the farmhouse. Outside the door she paused and took a deep breath before entering the kitchen. As soon as there was a lull in the conversation, she caught Nick's eye.

'I've been tidying your room, Nick and there's some things you need to put away. Come and do it now, whilst it's on my mind.'

He made as if to protest but the look in her eyes made him think again and he meekly followed her up the stairs. 'You've no right going into my room!' he protested.

'I wouldn't have to, if you kept it tidy! But that's not what I want to discuss. It's these!' she showed him the jacket and the CDs.

Nick's shoulders sagged. 'It was a dare,' he muttered.

'A dare! You stole for a dare?'

'Well, you have to . . . or the other lads laugh at you!'

'You could try getting new friends!'

'Yeh, well, I thought if I leave school I'd be leaving them, too . . . but now I'm thinking of staying on. Maybe trying to get in the Sixth Form College, or something like that. I didn't want to steal the things, Ros, honest I didn't! But some of the lads said they'd beat me up if I didn't!'

Ros could see real regret in his face but knew she couldn't be too soft with him. 'They'll have to go back, Nick. You can't keep them. I'll come with you, if you like . . . only it will have to be towards the end of the week, when I come back from France.'

It was a relief to wake up on Sunday morning. Surely everything bad that could happen had happened last week. Only the enquiry to face now . . . and then, hopefully, she could start to face the future again.

She was in two minds whether or not to go to church. She felt sure Paul would try to encourage her to confide in him and now, with even more secrets to hide, she didn't think that was a wise thing to do. It would be better to wait until everything was sorted and then make a clean breast of it.

In the end, she went. Eileen wanted them to go together as a family and so they did. Paul's sermon was on 'loving thy neighbour as you love yourself'. When Paul said that 'our neighbour is anyone with whom we come into contact,' Nick reddened, feeling sure Paul must know about the goods he had stolen from their 'neighbouring' town.

She had truly meant to avoid Martin, but he must have been only a few paces behind her leaving the church because, just as she reached the lych gate, he spoke her name as he grasped hold of her arm.

Ros turned swiftly. 'Martin! I'm sorry, but I've nothing to say to you right now.'

'Look, I'm sorry about the other night, the way it ended and all that. You've every right to be annoyed. I told Dad at the outset that it was a bit underhand but he wouldn't listen. He . . . '

Ros's temper, already simmering under what she imagined Paul's condemnation, flared into life. 'A bit underhand!' she snapped, dragging her arm out of his grip. 'Is that what you call it? You're despicable! You're . . . '

She involuntarily glanced past his shoulder and could see Paul looking their way, but she was too far away to read his expression and couldn't help feeling that she had once again slipped down a level in his estimation. She brushed at her arm as if she didn't want the slightest lingering of Martin's touch to remain on her.

'No doubt you will be hearing more from us about all this,' she said tight-lipped. 'No! Don't say another word. It will only make matters worse and I have enough to worry about right now. Please, excuse me.'

As soon as lunch was over, Ros packed her flight bag and was ready when Paul arrived to drive her to the airport. Just before she hurried out of the door to join him she thought better of leaving her mother totally ignorant of the dispute with Feltons. It would be just like Martin to come while she was away and try to wriggle out of his actions.

So, she said lightly to Eileen, 'I've good reason to think that the Feltons had something to do with the stream being flooded. Martin made a sort of apology about it, but don't let it worry you, Mum. And, if he comes round here whilst I'm away, tell him he'll have to wait until I get back. OK?'

'Eh, love! You must be mistaken, I'm sure! I've known Geoffrey most of my life. He wouldn't do anything like that.'

'Well, someone did. The branches

were cut, not broken. And Martin admitted it. Anyway, I must go. Paul's waiting.' She kissed her mother's cheek. 'Bye-bye! I'll see you Wednesday at the latest.'

As soon as she'd gone, Eileen picked up the phone.

9

Ros felt very tense on the way to the airport. She was very conscious of Paul at her side and knew that her feelings towards him were growing deeper. Who would have thought she would fall in love with a vicar?

She remembered nothing of the drive to the airport. Had Paul tried to make conversation? If so, she hadn't been aware of it, so deep had she been in the misery of her recollections. She glanced at him and he partly turned to smile at her.

'We're nearly there,' he said quietly, and turned back to look where he was driving. When he had parked the car he turned sideways in the driving seat and took hold of her hand, stroking it gently with his thumb.

'Something is very wrong, isn't it, Ros? Can't you share it with me? I'd like to feel that you could trust me.'

Ros looked up at him. Was it love for her she could see shining in his eyes? Oh, she wanted to deserve that love, but what if she were found guilty? What would happen? How could she inflict herself with such a stained reputation on this lovely man?

'Is it something to do with the man you met at the airport last week? Are you in some sort of trouble with him?' Paul asked gently.

Ros was surprised. 'How did . . . ?'

'Joanna wasn't exactly quiet in her condemnation of you,' he said with a wry grimace and then added quickly, 'You don't have to tell me, if you'd rather not. It won't change anything.'

But it might, Ros thought sadly. 'It . . . it does concern him,' she admitted quietly.

'Is he married?'

'What?' Her face flamed as the question hit her. 'Oh, no, nothing like that! He's a teacher at the school I taught at.'

She glanced at her watch and bit her lower lip. Time had flown. She clasped Paul's hand. 'I do want to tell you, Paul. I wish I'd told you at the very beginning, before . . . ' She wanted to say, 'before I fell in love with you' but bit back the words and, instead, just added, 'but there's not enough time. I've to report at the flight desk in five minutes. I will tell you, though, as soon as I get back. I owe you that much.'

Paul shook his head. 'You don't owe me anything, Ros. I just want to help you.'

She opened the car door and began to get out, then impulsively twisted back and leaned forward, intending to kiss his unsuspecting cheek, but Paul anticipated the movement and grasped hold of her shoulders, drawing her close, firmly kissing her lips.

She felt a longing to respond, but knew it would prolong the parting and she would miss her flight, so she stifled the response and drew away.

She got out of the car and began to

hurry towards the departure terminal. 'Text me with the time of your flight back!' Paul called after her . . . and she wasn't sure if it was her own thoughts echoing through her mind but she thought she heard him call, 'I love you!'

The hearing began at ten o'clock the following day. To begin with, everyone concerned was in the same large room. Here, it was explained that this wasn't a trial, but was an enquiry into the events leading up to the tragic accident and the accident itself.

Ros knew that the boys' parents were there and she could feel their eyes turn towards her and move on to Jerome Brest.

Ros kept her eyes on the chief investigator's face. She was glad she couldn't see Jerome's face . . . nor he see hers. Then they were told that all witnesses were to leave the room and were to wait in separate rooms where directed. They would be called in turn to speak of their part in the event and to say what they had seen.

At last, just after three o'clock, she was summoned back to the enquiry, where the chief investigator asked her if she were comfortable with the proceedings being in French. To which she replied, 'Oui, monsieur.'

Carefully, she went over the events, from Jerome's phone call late on the evening before the river trip to the tragedy itself, voicing her own feelings of inadequacy when the boys got into trouble. Sometimes, the investigator interrupted to ask more detailed questions or to request further explanation of something and Ros did her best to recall every moment correctly, trying not to breakdown when she heard a sob from one of the mothers.

'You make no mention of monsieur Brest asking you to telephone the meteorological office, mademoiselle Mansell?'

Ros swallowed. 'No, monsieur. He didn't. He simply told me to be there in time to help to check the students in as they arrived.'

'What about at an earlier briefing? I understand this trip had been planned over a period of time.'

'The phone call was my only briefing. As I said earlier, I was included at the last minute when another member of staff was unable to go.'

'And at no time did monsieur Brest ask you to make the weather check?'

'No, monsieur.'

'And do you have any personal regrets as to your performance in the event, mademoiselle?'

Ros hesitated. She had plenty, but they were all in the light of knowledge after the event.

'I regret not being to locate the boys earlier in the river; maybe I should have dived in more quickly or searched for longer.' She shook her head at the memory of being hauled out of the river by others and restrained from going back in. 'But I was exhausted by then.' She turned to face the two sets of parents. 'I'm sorry! I did my best, but I failed! I'm sorry!'

She was unaware that tears were streaming down her cheeks until someone seated next to her offered her a tissue. She took it gratefully and dabbed at her eyes, thankful when she heard the investigator tell her that was all for now. She could return to her hotel and come back at ten o'clock the next morning to face further questioning.

She felt very nervous the following day. Quietly, she reaffirmed her statement of the previous day, wondering whom they would believe . . . and what would happen to her if they believed Jerome's version of events.

She was thankful when she was allowed to step down and was escorted back to the waiting room. About an hour later, she was asked to proceed to another room and was there left alone. A few minutes later, the door opened and, to her consternation, Jerome came into the room. He seemed taken aback, but recovered more swiftly than she did.

Glancing back to make sure the door

was shut, he strode towards her, his face twisted with rage. 'Well. thanks for nothing!' he snarled bitterly. 'You couldn't even tell one small lie to save me from professional ruin, could you! I'll see you ruined, believe me!'

As he spoke the last words. his hand shot out and slapped hard against her head. Trying to dodge the blow, she stepped backwards, but the blow sent her off balance and she fell against a chair and on to the floor, her face catching the edge of the table. The pain knocked her sick.

Jerome took another step forward to Ros when a voice behind him said, 'That will do, monsieur Brest!' and he was hustled from the room.

Due to the altercation with Jerome, it was late on Thursday afternoon when Ros arrived back in England. To her disappointment. it wasn't Paul who met her at the airport, but Martin. She halted abruptly, then made as if to walk past him, her eyes still searching for Paul.

'What on earth's happened to you?' Martin demanded, grasping hold of her arm as she tried to pass by him.

She had completely forgotten the vivid bruising on her face, but she had no intention of telling Martin about the enquiry, not before she had told Paul and her mother.

'I had a slight altercation with a table,' she said lightly.

'Some table!' Martin quipped. 'I hope it looks as bad as you do!'

'Not even a scratch! Where's Paul?'

'He couldn't make it, and asked me to stand in for him. Something about going shopping with Nick. Bit of a let-down, isn't it, being stood up for your own kid brother.'

Ros felt a stab of apprehension. Had Paul somehow found out about Nick's shop-lifting? Was he doing what she should have been doing? Well, at least Paul's standing in the community should assist Nick in his plea for forgiveness! But did Paul think she had condoned Nick's actions by not insisting on returning the goods straightaway? Did their mum know?

'Oh, dear! I'd better get home straightaway.'

Martin raised an eyebrow. 'You're willing to get in my car now, are you?'

Ros's face reddened. 'Yes, but only because I've no option. I haven't forgotten what you've been doing.'

Martin took her flight bag out of her hand and turned to lead the way to his car. 'Let's get this straight, Ros! I didn't block your stream and I didn't damage the hedge. I might deserve your scorn for sweet-talking my way into your confidences, but I've done nothing illegal, nor has my father. Your mother believes me, even if you don't.'

'Mum?' She halted in her tracks. 'I knew you'd go round there as soon as I was out of the way, trying to wangle your way out of it!'

'I didn't go to your farm. Your mother phoned my father and they've sorted it out between them . . . at least, they've made some preliminary moves.

And anyway, you misunderstood my apology. I wasn't confessing to vandalism.'

He took hold of her arm and set her moving again.

'Well, what was it, then? What else had you to apologise about?'

Martin grimaced. 'I'm not very proud of myself, but Dad talked me into getting friendly with you so that we could see how the land lay, and that's an unintentional pun, about what your mother was planning to do about the farm. He wants to extend our land and . . . '

' . . . thought he'd make life difficult for us.'

'Don't you ever listen? We had nothing to do with the damage. Someone else must have done that, if indeed it was done deliberately.'

He tossed her flight bag on to the back seat and opened the passenger door for her. Ros slid into the seat, thinking about what Martin had said. She supposed it had to be true. It would have been out of character for Geoffrey Felton to break the law like that, so who had done the damage?

'Anyway, I'm sorry if I misled you or hurt you in any way,' Martin continued, as he slipped into first gear and began to drive away. 'You didn't strike me as being too over-enamoured by my advances, so I didn't think you'd really mind. I was more concerned with upsetting Joanna. I nearly ruined it there, I can tell you!'

'Joanna?'

'Yes. It was Joanna I was meeting when you said you'd seen me at the station in Shrewsbury the day you arrived . . . and I was with her at the airport when you were there with that French man. We'd . . . er . . . been away for a few days.'

Realisation dawned. 'Oh! So, it was you she was warning me off, was it? I thought she meant Paul!'

Martin raised an eyebrow. 'It didn't exactly stop you, then?'

Ros managed a lop-sided grin. 'All's

fair in love and war! I reckoned that it was one-sided on Joanna's part and if Paul hadn't made his intentions clear to her before I came on the scene, then there was nothing to prevent me responding to his moves.'

'So you've fallen for our handsome new vicar. I suppose I ought to feel a bit slighted — that you've fallen for his charms instead of mine.' He pursed his lips thoughtfully. 'I wonder what it's like going out with a vicar?'

Ros pulled a wry expression. The situations her family had found themselves in might mean that she'd never know. She wished she'd had the courage to confide in Paul earlier on. He would have done all he could to support her, she knew. How could she face him now, with her lack of trust standing between them?

Still, that was nothing to do with Martin, and she wasn't going to confide her doubts and concern with him!

10

As they neared Melford Green, Ros was startled to see a grass-cutter busy at work in one of their fields.

'Stop the car!' she commanded, twisting round in her seat, staring through the rear window through which she could see the top of the high chute and mown grass being blown into the collecting wagon at its side.

Martin drew to a standstill and Ros turned to face him. 'How on earth has Mum managed that?' she puzzled her thoughts out loud.

Martin's face had a look of rueful embarrassment. 'Part of the deal she's made with my father,' he admitted. 'No firm commitment until your silage is in. Knows how to drive a bargain, does your mother!'

Ros opened her mouth to speak but closed it again.

Martin grinned and set the car in motion again. Neither of them spoke until he pulled up by the farm gate. 'Safely delivered, mademoiselle!' he quipped with an exaggerated air of gallantry. He made as if to open his door but Ros forestalled him.

'I can manage, thank you,' she said a little ungraciously. 'Thanks for the lift. Just give me time to get my flight bag.'

'See you on Saturday,' Martin said by means of farewell, adding, 'at Eileen's surprise party,' as she looked at him blankly. 'We are invited, aren't we? Hope you've sweetened your temper by then.'

Ros made her way to the farmhouse, finding her mother in the kitchen baking a batch of fresh bread. Eileen's welcoming smile turned to a look of shock as she saw the state of Ros's face.

'Eh, Ros my love! Whatever has happened?'

She held out her arms and enveloped Ros within them, breaking Ros's determined self-control. Ros wept tears of relief that her ordeal was over, grateful for the timeless comfort of her mother's shoulder. When the flow began to diminish, she drew back and, over a welcome mug of coffee and a few homemade biscuits, told her mother about the tragic accident and the subsequent events and her fears for her future.

'You should have told me, love,' Eileen chastised her gently. 'I'd have understood. We'd all have stood by you.'

'I couldn't tell you, Mum. You'd just had a heart attack and I was afraid of upsetting you. I wanted to get it sorted before I said anything.'

'And is it sorted?' Eileen asked anxiously.

Ros nodded. 'Yes. There will be a letter of confirmation in a few days time. I can either go back there or apply for a teaching job in England. Or, even work here on the farm, if that would help.'

Eileen reached out her hand to touch

Ros's arm, but shook her head at Ros's offer. 'No, Ros. That's not the answer. I've given everything a lot of thought over the past few months and more so over the last few days. We can't go on as we are. No, don't disagree just yet. I know what people have been saying recently, that we can't manage . . . and, much as I hate to admit it, they're right. I've not been managing for months now, a year maybe. The work's too much.'

'But, Mum, we can't just give up.'

'No, but we can diversify. I've been giving it a bit of thought, but I suppose I wanted to hang on to see if you wanted to come back full time. But, you don't really, do you, in spite of your offer just now? Be honest, now.'

Ros reached out to touch her mum's hand. 'Not really. I don't mind the hens and even a few sheep, but even after all these years, the cows still terrify me a bit. I'd rather work with people any day, especially with children. I enjoy teaching.'

'And Nick certainly doesn't want to farm. I wouldn't listen to him because I didn't want to face the facts. Eh, all three of you take after your dad. He never liked farming either. He only came into it because of me. He would have preferred to do something like organising and conducting adventure holidays . . . like what Caroline's gone off doing.'

'I'm sorry, Mum.'

'Nay, lass. We are what we are, and farming isn't what it was.'

'But what will we do, Mum? I know Geoffrey Felton wants some of the land, but I doubt he wants all of it and where would we live if we sold the house?'

'Now that's what I'd like to talk about. I've always wanted to run a Bed and Breakfast here, but Ted put an end to that hope when he left. So, how about if that's what we do now? We can sell those top fields to Geoffrey and with the money raised there, convert the barn attached to the house into a modern dwelling. I had plans drawn up years ago.'

Eileen's eyes sparkled as she talked, removing any doubts from Ros's mind that their mum might simply be making the best of a bad job.

'And I'm sure we'll get planning permission to change the cow-shed into holiday cottages,' she continued. 'That would leave us with the two large barns down the yard and the hens and ducks.'

Ros shook her head in amazement. 'I think it's wonderful! But where does Geoffrey Felton come in? What started you off approaching him? Martin said he didn't come round to pester you.'

'No, he didn't. After what you said just as you were leaving the other day, I got on to the phone as soon as you'd gone to see what it was all about. Geoffrey denied any involvement in blocking the stream etc, and I believe him. He said he wants to open a golf course on his land, but needs extra acreage. He just wanted Martin to find out how we felt about things before approaching me on the subject.

'So, there we are. If you and Nick and Debbie agree with me, we can go right ahead and put everything in the hands of our solicitors, and all we have to get through in the next few weeks is managing the cows until we sell them. Talking of which,' she added, glancing at the clock, 'do you feel up to giving Hugh a hand with the milking? Claire's mum was picking Katie-Anne up from school and keeping her to play with Claire for a while. I'll send her down to help with the eggs as soon as she comes home.'

Ros went down to the milking parlour, where she found Hugh starting the milking process.

'Your back better, is it?' she asked with a sceptical smile.

'Comes and goes, it does,' Hugh said blatantly. 'Missed me, did you? I knew you would! It's like I keep telling you, your mam can't manage the farm as it is. Needs to cut back she does.'

Ros didn't reply but went over to the

second aisle, leaving Hugh to see to the first side. They had nearly finished when Katie-Anne came rushing in, her face upset. 'Ros! Ros! The duck eggs are broken! It wasn't me, honestly. I was going to turn them, only they were already broken!'

Ros straightened up. 'Oh, no! Will you finish off here, Hugh? I'd better go and see what's happened.'

She ran after Katie-Anne, catching up with her in the doorway to the dairy. One glance at the incubator brought a smile to her face.

'Oh! They're hatching, Katie-Anne. See, it's the duckling who is cracking the shell with its beak! See! There goes another one! Oh, isn't it exciting!'

Katie-Anne jumped up and down, watching as the shells cracked more and more. Eventually, the one farthest along the process split and the wet bedraggled feathers of the duckling could be plainly seen.

'It is all right?' Katie-Anne asked anxiously. 'It doesn't look very well.'

'Its feathers will soon dry out. Then it will look fine. Stay and watch for a while longer while I take the cows up to pasture.'

She hurried back to the milking parlour and stopped dead in the doorway. Hugh was pouring a churn of milk down the drain!

'Whatever are you doing, Hugh?' she gasped. 'Stop it at once. That's perfectly good milk!'

Startled, he dropped the churn and the rest of its contents spilled on to the floor. 'Nay! Nay!' he blustered. 'It were contaminated! One o' t' cows' udders bled into it!'

'Which one?' Ros demanded. 'Let me see it!'

'Well, I've wiped it now! I've fixed it!' he said belligerently.

'You've done this before, haven't you?' Ros accused. 'That's why our milk yield has been falling. You've been pouring some if it away, you nasty old man!'

'Don't you be calling me names,

missy! You can't prove nothing and I'll sue you for slander, as well as for flood damage to my land!'

Ros paused suddenly as a flash of realisation came to her. Her eyes narrowed. 'Oh, I don't know,' she said thoughtfully. 'I reckon the police could soon match up the saw marks on those branches. We've kept them, you know.'

She almost laughed at the sudden alarmed expression that flitted into his eyes. Not that he was ready to admit defeat.

'Bah! You can't prove anything!' he blustered. 'Too dark a night. It was, see! You'll have a fine job planting that on me!' A crafty gleam shone in his eyes. 'I tell you what! You forget about this milk and I'll forget about yon damage to my land. How about that? That's a fair offer, isn't it?'

Ros laughed harshly. 'I don't think so!' She held up her hand to cut short his protestations of innocence. 'It's all 'water under the bridge' if you'll forgive the pun, Hugh. The fact is we've decided to take your advice, after all. We're going to sell part of the farm.'

His eyes lit up. 'When? You'll give me first option, won't you? I'm still willing to do a deal with your mam. A few acres along this side, including the stream, and the acres over yonder beyond the river,' he added nonchalantly. 'Course, the land's not up to much. Been neglected for too long, but I'll see you all right, I will.'

'The acres adjoining Felton land? You'd have no access.'

A glimmer of understanding came to her. The crafty old devil! He must have got wind of Geoffrey wanting to buy some land and hoped to do a deal with him later, with their land. She decided to bring it to an end. 'Sorry, Hugh. We've already got a buyer.'

'Who? Who are you dealing with? Maybe I can match him?'

'I doubt it, Hugh. He's giving us top price.'

His face fell, but he wasn't quite ready to give up. 'What about the land this side, then? You won't be wanting the stream if you're giving up farming!'

'We're not giving up completely, but I tell you what, Hugh. Tell your solicitor to get in touch and we'll see what we can do about granting you limited access . . . at a fair price of course!'

Bursting into the kitchen to tell Eileen about Hugh's treachery, Ros pulled up in amazement at the rapturous expression on her mother's face.

'Mum?'

Eileen dazedly handed her the phone, stretching out her arms to Katie-Anne and sweeping her into an ecstatic embrace. 'He's found her, love! Your daddy's found Caroline and her friend! They're already on their way home! They'll be here by tea-time on Saturday!'

Ros half-heard her mother and her uncle at the same time. Ken was jubilant.

'And isn't it Eileen's fiftieth birthday on Saturday?' he asked Ros. 'Have you got anything planned, because I've got an extra present for her!'

Ros held her breath as she listened, saying at length, 'I'll give you my mobile phone number, Uncle Ken. Ring me tomorrow and I'll tell you where we're going.'

Their euphoria over Ken's news was shattered by a phone call twenty minutes later. It was from the Shrewsbury constable with the news that Nick was being held in custody overnight and would be appearing before a magistrate the following morning.

After reluctantly telling her mother what she knew of Nick's proposed activities that afternoon, Ros picked up the phone again.

'I'm surprised Paul hasn't telephoned us,' she said over her shoulder as she began to dial his number. 'He should be able to tell us more details.'

There was no answer.

Ros pursed her lips as she wondered what to do next. The officer who had phoned them had declared himself unable to disclose any further details.

Maybe Paul would call on his way home? She tried his mobile phone but with no success.

When the phone rang ten minutes later, Ros pounced on it before her mother could rise from her chair. 'Paul? What's happened?'

'Sorry to disappoint you again, Ros,' came Martin's voice. 'Dad's just had a call from our upright young vicar. You're not going to believe this, but he has been arrested and is being held in police custody overnight!'

11

'What? I don't believe you!' Ros gasped. 'Why should Paul be arrested?'

'Ah, now. You're not going to like this bit. Your Nick was involved along with a gang of lads from the High School. 'Public brawling' was the term used, so I heard!'

'Brawling? Paul? I don't believe you! This isn't funny, Martin! Mum's extremely worried about Nick. We knew he had been arrested. I thought it was . . . ' She snapped her lips together. The fewer people who knew about the shoplifting the better.

Martin didn't seem to have noticed her broken sentence. He made an exaggerated sigh. 'Not funny indeed. I wonder what Paul will preach about on Sunday? Turning the other cheek, do you think? No, hardly appropriate. Dear, dear! He has fallen from grace!'

'Not at all!' Ros said sharply. 'Knowing Paul, he would only get involved in fighting with good intentions! He must have been provoked!'

Or helping Nick, she inwardly surmised. Oh, dear!

Martin's voice sobered. 'You're probably right. I was only teasing. Anyway, he was only allowed one phone call and he phoned Dad as he's the Church Warden and asked him to pass on the information to you . . . only he had to go out to a meeting. Paul also said not to go to the hearing. You could be there all day waiting for your turn and he knows how busy you are on the farm. He'll bring Nick home as soon as he can and explain what happened.'

And with that, Ros and Eileen had to be content.

Friday seemed to be an endless day. Not surprisingly, Hugh didn't put in an appearance, so Ros had to struggle with the milking by herself, whilst Eileen saw to the hens and collecting the eggs. Claire's mother had taken Katie-Anne to school again and said she was welcome to stay for tea and she would bring her home in time for bed ... much to Ros and Eileen's relief, knowing it wouldn't be long before the village was buzzing with the news of the double arrest.

Ros felt in turmoil. Her anxiety over Nick and Paul's arrest was intensified by her concern over what the affair might do to her budding relationship with Paul. The bishop would have to be informed.

It was mid-afternoon before Paul's car pulled up outside the farm and Nick got out to open the gate. Ros had only just completed what should have been the morning's work and was pouring some boiling water into the teapot when Nick came into the kitchen with Paul hesitantly following.

'Eh, Nick, love!' Eileen greeted her son, her arms open wide, welcoming him home.

Ros looked past them, her shocked eyes taking in Paul's bruised face. His

left eye was puffed and almost closed.
Her fingers flew to touch her lower lip.
'Paul!'

She wanted to rush across the
kitchen and hold his face between her
hands, to soothe the bruises with her
fingertips . . . or even her lips. She
might have done so had Paul's expression given her the slightest sign that
such a move would be welcome. But it
didn't.

He looked dazed.

Maybe her instinctive feelings of
tenderness had been obvious by the
expression in her eyes. If so, had it
repelled him? He stood immobile in the
doorway, looking at her over Eileen and
Nick.

'Ros! What's happened? Maybe I
should have gone to France with you
and tried my luck there! You look as
though you could have done with an
extra pair of fists.'

He tried to speak lightly, but his attempt
at humour sounded falsely jovial and
even Paul winced at his own words.

'I . . . fell against a table,' Ros said, with a sidelong warning glance towards her mother.

'And your business in France? It was successfully accomplished?'

Ros knew she was being held at arms' length and was aware that a faint flush was creeping up her neck and over her face. She swallowed hard as she nodded, inwardly berating herself for still not opening her heart to him . . . but, how could she?

'Yes,' she choked. 'Perfectly, thank you.'

'Good.'

Ros sensed that an inner battle was going on . . . but, looking clearly embarrassed, he still didn't move towards her.

'It's good to see you back, Ros. I'm sorry I couldn't meet you and that your return had to coincide with our little brush with the law! I didn't do a very good job of helping Nick, I'm afraid.'

'No.'

What else could she say? Fortunately,

Eileen came to her rescue.

'Now, come on. Let's sit down at the table while Ros pours out the tea. Paul, you can make yourself useful by putting some of these scones on to a plate. And, Nick, get the butter out of the larder and bring a nice jar of jam.'

The activity covered the momentary embarrassment and Eileen waited until mugs of tea had been poured before she spoke again. 'Now, who's going to start the ball rolling? It had better be you, Nick. Whatever were you thinking about, stealing things like that?'

Nick flushed red. 'I'm sorry, Mum. I didn't want to do it. I just wanted to be one of the lads. I felt no-one understood what I was going through. Missing Dad and not wanting to stay in farming. I wanted to take the things back, but Gary said the lads would kill me! I knew they wouldn't, really . . . but they'd beat me up. And they did.'

'So, how did you get drawn into it, Paul? Did you just happen to be there?

Here, tuck in, lad!' offering him the plate of scones.

Paul took one and placed it on his plate, but ended up crumbling it between his fingers rather than buttering it and eating it.

'No. Nick had come to me and told me about the CDs and the leather jacket he'd stolen and, as he said, he wanted to take them back. So I said I would go with him. Unfortunately, I went in casual clothes and the manager of the shop didn't believe I'm a vicar and called the police.

'Meanwhile, some of the lads Nick was involved with were in the shop, stealing more goods. When they realised what Nick was doing, they launched into him and soon had him on the ground, kicking him.'

He looked embarrassed again. 'I'm afraid I saw red and joined in, trying to drag them off Nick . . . so I was right in the thick of it when the police arrived. Someone grabbed me from behind and I thrust my elbow back into his face, only to realise too late that I'd assaulted an officer!'

Ros clapped a hand to her mouth. 'You hit a policeman! No wonder they locked you up!'

Paul grimaced. 'Yes, I have a lot to live down! I'd better make 'forgiveness' the issue of Sunday's sermon this week!'

'Are you in serious trouble over it?' Ros asked soberly, her eyes flickering briefly to his, but wary of lingering there in case he saw the depth of her feelings.

Paul returned her glance with identical brevity. 'I might be . . . with the bishop . . . but, in the end, the magistrate accepted our version of the events. Nick has been committed to doing some Community Service, which I negotiated into helping me run the youth club.'

He seemed relieved to include Nick in his glance. 'And I got off with a warning about brawling in public places. Nick's pals didn't get off quite so lightly as they've been in trouble before. I'm afraid it's a Young Offenders' Detention Centre for Gary Wellings and a few of the others.'

He turned to face Eileen. 'I'm sorry to have let you down, Eileen. We were going to come clean about it when it was all over, when I optimistically thought I would have turned things around for Nick. A touch of misplaced pride, I suppose,' he ruefully criticised himself.

Eileen shook her head. 'Don't be too hard on yourself, lad. Your heart was in the right place. I'm sure you'll find everyone very supportive. Don't you think so, Ros?' drawing her daughter into the conversation.

Ros was feeling utterly miserable. This wasn't going at all as it had in her imagination, where Paul sweeping her into his arms murmuring sweet endearments had been more the order of things.

'Y . . . yes,' she stammered. 'I'm sure they will. You have done nothing to reproach yourself with. I'm sure no-one will censure you.'

Paul looked around at the three Mansells, each one of them showing signs of discomfort. 'Well, I think I'd better be getting back to the vicarage and leave you to get on with things here. I know how busy you'll be soon, with the afternoon milking,' he excused his leaving to Eileen. 'Thanks for the tea and don't be too hard on Nick. I think he's learned his lesson, haven't you, young man?'

Nick hung his head. 'Yeh. Sorry, Mum. I have, honestly. I won't do it again. But, you won't make me stay in farming because of it, will you?'

'No, lad . . . but that's something else we need to talk about.'

'And I'll see you at the youth club tonight, will I?' Paul asked him.

'What? Tonight? I thought . . . '

'No point in putting it off. Everyone will know all about our escapade — the outcome, if not the reason.' He laughed nervously. 'And I would genuinely be grateful for your support.'

Nick grinned at Paul's admission. 'Oh, well, in that case, you're on . . . mate!' Paul laughed as they exchanged a high hand-slap.

'Good. I'll see you later, then. 'Bye for now.'

And to Ros's mixed emotions of sorrow and relief, he left.

Later, over their evening meal, Nick spoke more about the events in his life the previous day and Ros told him about the reason for her brief return to France . . . but, once the meal had been cleared away, Eileen suggested she made another pot of tea and that the three of them sit at the table to discuss the future of the farm.

Later, when Eileen was seeing to putting Katie-Anne to bed, Ros brought Nick up-to-date with Uncle Ken's latest phonecall, asking him to make sure that Paul was aware of the extra guests at Eileen's party the following day.

By the time Nick was ready to set off to the youth club, he was lighter in heart than he had been for many a month.

★   ★   ★

'Are you ready, Mum? It's time we were off!'

Ros was nervous with suppressed excitement. Her heart was thumping at an alarming rate and she just hoped it wasn't all going to be too much for Eileen to cope with!

'But what about Ken and Caroline?' Eileen objected. 'They're not here yet. They won't know where to find us.'

'Yes, they will. He rang me on my mobile from the airport. Caroline had my number. I've told them where to go.'

'Which is more than you've told me! Are you up to something, Ros Mansell?'

'Who, me?' Ros asked innocently. 'Of course not! And we've to pick Katie-Anne up from the vicarage, remember.'

'So, who is this unexpected visitor of Paul's? The one whose daughter Katie-Anne is playing with?'

'Someone he met a few weeks ago. Don't worry.'

Ros parked by the vicarage and went inside, only to re-emerge a few minutes later with a pile of boxes in her hands. 'His housekeeper says they're at the village hall and would we take these boxes there? Here, have them on your knee. You can help me carry them.'

A few minutes later they were going up the steps into the hall. 'Hold the door open for Mum, Nick,' Ros commanded, stepping aside to let Eileen go in first. 'In the main hall, she said, Mum!'

As Eileen opened the door into the main hall a loud cheer went up and Eileen's, 'Well, I never!' was drowned by a loud rendering of 'Happy Birthday, To You!' being sung by the occupants of the crowded room.

What an evening!

The buffet table was laden with food and everyone was invited to tuck in and that speeches etc would come later with the toast and the cutting of the magnificent cake.

'So, where's that present you said you'd brought me, Ken?' Eileen asked, looking around at the assembled crowd with a happy glow in her heart.

'I thought you'd never ask!' Ken replied. 'It's in that room over there. It's too big for me to carry in here. You'd better go and see it. Go with her, Ros. She might need some help!'

Ros accompanied her mother to the door. They had put two comfortable armchairs in there earlier and, when she opened the door for her mother to pass through, she could see that the occupant of one of them, now getting to his feet, was looking as nervous as she was.

Ros stepped back and let Eileen pass in front of her.

Eileen stopped and stared. 'Well I never!' she said for the second time that evening. 'Ted Mansell, by all that's wonderful! And where have you been all this time? That was some holiday you took! I hope it was worth it!'

Ros heard her dad chuckle. 'It was . . . and it wasn't,' she heard him say. 'Will you have me back, Eileen?'

'You daft ha'porth! You know I will, or you wouldn't have come, would you?'

'I'd take the chance, love!'

'Eh, come here, then and give me a kiss.'

Ros felt two hands on her shoulders and turned to see Paul standing behind her. He gently ran his fingertips down her left cheek and said, 'We need to talk. Let's go outside into the garden. It's still quite warm out there.'

He took hold of her hand and they slipped through a doorway into the garden that linked the church hall with the vicarage. The scent of honeysuckle hung heavily in the air, Ros's heart was thumping wildly. She felt as though an electric current was running through their hands and the nearness of him made her feel weak with love for him.

A mixture of emotions coursed through her . . . regret that she hadn't yet confided in him about the reason she had left her teaching job in Paris, mixed with trepidation that Nick's slip into petty thieving made her unworthy of his love. He was going to risk ruining his career! She couldn't let him!

She stopped walking, making him halt also. 'Paul, you can't . . . '

As she began to speak, Paul placed his hands on her shoulders and drew her closer. 'Can't what?' he asked softly, gently stroking her bruised face again.

The spicy fragrance of his aftershave wafted over her, sending spirals of desire coursing through her.

'You can't . . . kiss me,' she whispered unconvincingly.

Her lips tingled in anticipation of his kiss and she knew that however unsuitable a prospect she might be, she was going to let him kiss her . . . just this once, so that she could live on the memory of it until her heart stopped aching with longing for him.

His lips felt like silk and all thoughts of resistance evaporated into the balmy air. Their bodies moulded together and Ros leaned into the strength of him, surrendering her weakness.

'You were saying?' Paul murmured against her lips, gently caressing them.

'The bishop mightn't like it.'

'I've no intention of kissing the bishop . . . only you!' and resumed the kiss, stifling the giggle that began to bubble deep in Ros's throat.

'Silly!' she said, when the kiss paused again. 'I meant he might think me unsuitable . . . and my delinquent brother! I'm sure you thought it, too.'

His surprise was genuine. 'Did I? When?'

'Yesterday, when you brought Nick home. I saw the hesitation in your face. You deliberately held back from me.'

'Oh, my darling girl! That was my guilt over losing my self-control when I joined in the fighting. You see. I actually enjoyed the scrap . . . and I felt compelled to offer my resignation to the bishop . . . and I didn't want to involve you in what might have been a painful 'sacking', a transfer at the very least, I thought. Plus the fact I'd failed because you couldn't confide in me.'

'Oh, you didn't fail me! It was me. I didn't want to risk you scorning me for my alleged neglect of duty. I thought it made me unsuitable as a prospective wife of a vicar. That is . . . ' She stopped in some confusion.

'Wife, did you say?' Paul said, grinning at her discomfort.

Then he kissed the tip of her nose. 'Actually, the bishop thinks you'll do rather well . . . and, to stop you worrying, Nick told me all about the French incident. My dearest love. What torment you must have gone through.'

He held her away from him and gently tilted her face towards him. 'Never keep anything like that from me again. We share everything, d'you hear?'

'Like you sharing your worry that I wouldn't want a failed vicar?' Ros murmured coyly, determined to let him know that he wasn't going to find her totally biddable.

'Touché!' Paul grinned. 'And no more about me being a 'failure'! Did Nick tell you that the youth club was a 'knock-out' last night? Apparently my 'public brawling' has raised my 'street cred' immensely. At least a dozen new lads came and seemed somewhat in awe of me.'

'Stunned, more like! You do look rather shocking . . . in a rugged sort of way.' Ros grinned at him, slipping out of the circle of his arms. 'Race you to the summerhouse!'

Paul caught up with her as she reached the rustic summerhouse that was basking in the early evening sun. Cushions were invitingly placed on a wicker two-seater settee.

'You planned this!' Ros accused him laughingly.

'Guilty, as charged.'

He drew her down beside him and gathered her in his arms. Ros melted against him as he kissed her forehead, her eyes, her neck and finally her lips with a depth of longing that thrilled her, stirring a responding joy.

Paul rested his elbow on the back of the settee and looked down at her. 'I love you,' he whispered. 'I want to marry you . . . soon!'

'I love you, too . . . and, if you're asking, yes, I'll marry you!'

Paul gave a delighted shout. 'When? Is August too soon?'

'The sooner the better, the way I feel right now!'

'Good! I'll get in touch with the bishop again!'

And they kissed again.

THE END

We do hope that you have enjoyed reading this large print book.

Did you know that all of our titles are available for purchase?

We publish a wide range of high quality large print books including:
**Romances, Mysteries, Classics
General Fiction
Non Fiction and Westerns**

Special interest titles available in large print are:
**The Little Oxford Dictionary
Music Book, Song Book
Hymn Book, Service Book**

Also available from us courtesy of Oxford University Press:
**Young Readers' Dictionary
(large print edition)
Young Readers' Thesaurus
(large print edition)**

For further information or a free brochure, please contact us at:
**Ulverscroft Large Print Books Ltd.,
The Green, Bradgate Road, Anstey,
Leicester, LE7 7FU, England.
Tel:** (00 44) **0116 236 4325**
Fax: (00 44) **0116 234 0205**

THE EAGLE STONE

Heather Pardoe

While assisting her father in selling provisions to visitors to the top of Snowdon, Elinor Owen meets the adventuress Lady Sara Raglan and her handsome nephew, Richard. Eli is swiftly drawn into Lady Sara's most recent adventure, becoming a spy for Queen Victoria's government. Now, up against the evil Jacques, Eli and Richard are soon fighting for their lives, while Lady Sara heads for a final showdown and pistols at dawn with Jacques on the summit of Snowdon itself.